THONGOR PITS HIS STRENGTH AGAINST THE EVIL SCIENCE OF ZAAR, THE CITY OF MAGICIANS

Thongor stares moodily at the power crystal, the glowing bit of stone that is to change the face of the earth and alter the path of the future. He must have more of them, if he is to protect his empire against the black sorcery of Zaar!

Then his mood of foreboding passes, and the zest of adventure fills his veins like heady wine. To venture again into the unknown vastness of the eastern plains! To seize a mighty weapon for defense within the very shadow of Zaar's ebon walls!

But all the while the strange, all-seeing Eye of Zaar watches. It is the beginning of the Last Battle. . . .

THONGOR
IN THE
CITY OF MAGICIANS

LIN CARTER

PAPERBACK LIBRARY, Inc.

New York

THONGOR IN THE CITY OF MAGICIANS
is dedicated to my friends
Gray Morrow
George Heap
and *Ken Beale*
—*kojans* of the Empire

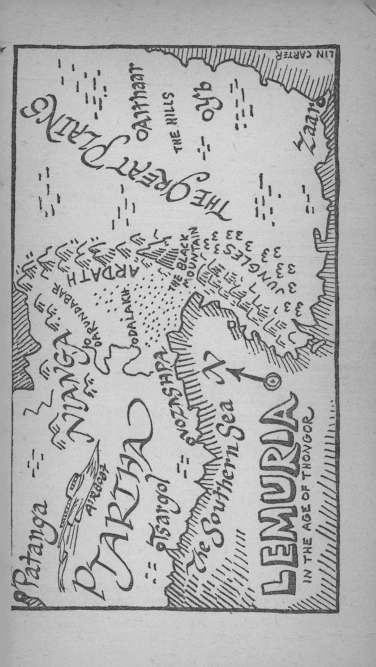

LIN CARTER

OATTHAAT

THE HILLS

OYB

THE GREAT PLAINS

Zaar

ARDATH

THE BLACK MOUNTAIN

JUNGLES

DARO PURNDABAR

ODALAKH

Patanga

NIANGA

AIRBOAT

PTARTHA

VOZASHPA

Tsargol

The Southern Sea

LEMURIA

IN THE AGE OF THONGOR

PROLOGUE

THONGOR THE MIGHTY
AND THE BLACK DRUIDS OF ZAAR

". . . Thus did Thongor the Barbarian whelm and drive forth from his lands the cruel, accursed, and demon-worshipping Druids who had long sought power over the Nine Cities of the West. But, in the years that followed, the ominous shadow of Zaar fell darkening from the remotest edge of the world, until it did imperil the bold young cities of the West. And on the Black Altars of Chaos the Nine Wizards of Zaar vowed a terrible vengeance against the warrior-king of Patanga who had crushed their brethren in the West. They swore with a dreadful oath that the Doom of Thongor should be so unspeakable that its memory would haunt the minds of men for untold ages yet to come."

—The Lemurian Chronicles

> One night as Thongor lay in sleep,
> His spirit soared aloft to stand
> On cliffy heights above the deep
> In some unknown and nameless land.
>
> To him the Gods appeared and told
> Of doom from Zaar, and bade him scan
> The book Sharajsha writ of old,
> Therein to seek the hope of man.

—Thongor's Saga, XVII, 1-2.

. . . THUS BEGINS THE LEGEND OF THE LAST BATTLE WHEREIN THE FATE OF MANKIND WAS DECIDED.

CHAPTER 1

SECRET CAVERN OF TREASURE

Sharajsha's secret book lies hid
Beneath the Temple buried deep,
Which like some mighty pyramid
Conceals the treasure it doth keep.

—*Thongor's Saga*, XVII, 3.

Night hung like a black curtain above the walled city of stone that stood at the mouth of the Twin Rivers. The darkness hid the great golden moon of ancient Lemuria behind a pall, and veiled from sight her attendant host of stars. Naught moved through the streets of Patanga the City of the Flame but the sighing night-wind and an occasional troop of archers on their way to relieve the guards stationed at the city's gates. But above the city, slim glittering flying boats of the Air Guard circled silently, keeping the watch.

They floated above the Great Plaza that lay at the heart of the stone metropolis, and above the domed roof of the huge Temple of Nineteen Gods that fronted on this central square, and above the mighty Thorian Way, that broad avenue which spanned the width of the city from the plaza to the frowning bastions of the Western Gate. Tirelessly they kept their lonely vigil, for Patanga was the heart of a vast empire, the Sarkonate of the Five Cities, and although its banners of black and gold fluttered above most of the cities along the gulf and down to the thunderous shores of Yashengzeb Chun the Southern Sea, many cunning and savage foes watched the rise of the young empire with envious eyes, and schemed to bring those banners down into the trodden dust.

But tonight, it seemed, those envious eyes slept, for the summer night was silent, and within the curve of the mighty walls, great Patanga slept secure.

But one there was who did not sleep.

Through the dark aisles of the Temple of Nineteen Gods, a lone figure prowled on silent feet. The high domed roof of the temple was murmurous with whispers, and below all was blackness, save for the eternal lights which flamed before the High Altar and the stupendous images of carven stone.

When his silent steps had brought him to the foot of this altar, the dark figure put out one hand and touched a hidden spring concealed amidst the symbolic designs wrought from the pale marble. A whisper of sound—and a black opening yawned!

Down a winding stair that coiled beneath the altar into a secret cavern whose very existence was known but to a few, passed the tall figure.

He emerged into the Grotto of the Flame.

A gigantic cavern lay before him, walls of ancient stone rising to a high-arched roof wherefrom hung dripping stalactites . . . thick spears of pearly stone as large as the fangs of Baroumphar, the Father of All Dragons in Lemurian fable. And the floor of the cavern rose to meet these dangling spears, rising in glassy humped stalagmites formed through countless aeons of slow calcareous dripping, endless centuries of mineral-laden ooze from the glistening stone spears overhead. A weird and terrible scene of primitive splendor!

But strangest of all was The Flame.

In the center of the cavern floor was a deep, low-lipped well, like some fantastic crater. From the black mouth of this sunken pit rose a mighty sheet of fire, emerald-green, its weird glow flickering and moving over the glassy forest of stalagmites and stalactites. . . . Strange was this ever-burning flame of emerald radiance! No mortal alive knew its secret. The Yellow Druids of Yamath, Lord of the Flame, that had ruled the City of Patanga before the coming of Thongor the Mighty, cloaked its curious nature in whispered myth. "The Ever-Burning One" they called it, and "The Eternal Fire."

Perhaps it was a jet of unknown vapor that rose from the secret heart of the Lemurian continent—or from the very bowels of the earth itself. For ages and ages beyond the memory of man The Flame had burned. Sharajsha, the

9

great wizard of Lemuria who lived no more, had once conjectured that it rose from the unknown volcanic world of fire that roared in supernal fury far below the bedrock of the continent. Within that labyrinthine world of hidden caverns, colossal forces seethed in unstable balance, held in check as yet, but with the eventual passages of unborn ages, destined to burst free in a thunderous fury of cataclysmic power whose convulsions would shatter and sink all of Lemuria beneath the foaming waves of the mighty Pacific . . . a watery grave from whence naught should be left of the splendor and glory of the first brave kingdoms of Man but a fragment of legend, and a name . . . *Lemuria, the Lost Continent, the Cradle of Man.*

Grim-faced, Thongor looked upon The Flame. It was he, the Lord of the Five Cities, who had come down the secret stair into these subterranean crypts by a hidden way the old sorceror, Sharajsha, had revealed to him years before. It was he, the Sark-of-Sarks, the Emperor, who waked and roamed while his people slept.

A great bronze lion of a man was Thongor of the Northlands, thewed like a savage god, his splendid body bare save for a loincloth of crimson cloth and the jeweled leather harness of a Lemurian warrior, an affair of buckled straps that crisscrossed his brawny chest, whereto were clipped with brass rings the scabbard of a dirk and the great Valkarthan broadsword that never left his side.

His grim, impassive face was majestic and stern beneath the rude mane of coarse thick black hair that poured over his massive back and shoulders and was held from his scowling black brows by a circlet of red gold set with square-cut black opals from the mountain-mines of Mommur. Clipped with cairngorm brooches to the wide collar of black leather that circled his corded throat, a huge crimson cloak swung from his broad shoulders. Gold rings flashed in the emerald light from arm and sinewy wrist. His square, stern jaw was grim-set, and his strange golden eyes were without expression as he stared at the flickering, dancing glory of The Flame.

But it was not to consult the ancient oracle of The Flame that Thongor visited by night these secret caverns. He strode across the cavern floor towards the further wall, boot-heels ringing on the cold wet stone, the crimson cloak belling out behind him like the wings of some fantastic bird as he strode on.

It was *fear* that kept Thongor from his rest, fear that had roused him from his place beside his sleeping princess and goaded him forth into the mysterious night—fear for his people, and dread of what the future might hold for them.

Thongor was a barbarian, the last survivor of his savage and primitive tribe, the Blackhawk Clan of Valkarth, whose rock-built stronghold fronted on the cold foam of Zharanga Tethrabaal, the Great North Ocean. He had come down from the bleak and savage wilds of the Northlands, down across the Mountains of Mommur into the lush and jungle-clad hills of the South where glittering young cities reared bright towers against the morning sky . . . to the South, with its young nations and ancient evils, where the kingly ambitions of sark and the priestly greed of druid strove one against the other for supremacy.

With the indomitable strength of a young giant and the matchless fighting skill of one raised from the cradle with a sword in his hand, Thongor had brawled and guzzled, roistered and fought, swaggered and wandered through half the cities of the South. First as thief and assassin, bandit and vagabond, then as galley-slave at the oarlocks of Shembis, sweating beneath the cruel lash. Next as pirate chieftain, ravishing the seaport cities along the Patangan Gulf. Later, through his comradeship with a young warrior named Ald Turmis, he had worn the scarlet leather of a mercenary swordsman, and rode to war with the scarlet-and-black dragon banners of Thurdis streaming above his helm and a red sword in one brawny fist.

In those wild and bloody swashbuckling days, he gave no thought to the morrow and what it might bring. Nor had he any desires that could not be sated with a cup of red wine or a willing pair of scarlet lips or a keen-edged sword to cut a crimson path through the thundering battlefields of the wide-wayed world.

But the wise gods of ancient Lemuria, or that destiny that some say rules even the gods, had a strange fate reserved for the shaggy-maned barbarian from the savage Northlander steppes. First, his feet were set on a wandering path that led him on a fantastic quest halfway across the

11

breadth of Lemuria to the Inland Sea of Neol-Shendis, where with the mighty wizard Sharajsha by his side he battled with the very lightning of the gods in his hands for weapon in a cosmic duel against the last of the reptilian Dragon Kings who had ruled the planet for long ages before the coming of the First Men. And in this fantastic adventure, whose memory, carried down the whispered byways of saga and legend, was to outlast the very continent, he befriended the gorgeous young girl who was to become his mate—Sumia, exiled Princess of Patanga the City of Fire. Driven from her throne by the vulpine greed of Vaspas Ptol, the Yellow Archdruid who had seized the royal power on the death of her father, the Princess Sumia had found for her champion Thongor, the mightiest warrior of his world.

Thongor's unconquerable courage and fighting prowess had smashed the army of Sumia's foes, overwhelmed the Yellow Druids and drove them forth from the land, liberated the City of the Flame and restored Sumia to her ancient throne—and Thongor took his place at her side as sark, or king, of the land of Patanga.

But with his royal title, Thongor also took on a host of troubles and tasks. For Patanga was ringed in with powerful enemies. Other cities, such as seacoast Tsargol to the south, and warlike Thurdis across the Gulf, rose to contend with the barbarian conqueror. Many times in the six years since wise old Eodrym, Hierarch of the Temple of Nineteen Gods, had wed Thongor and his Princess before the altars of Father Gorm, had the war-trumpets rung out and the Sark of Patanga had thundered with his legions to the fields of war. Thurdis the City of the Dragon had fallen before his sword, and Shembis by the gulf, and Tsargol to the south, that fronted on the main. Thus had he built a mighty Empire, placing his dearest comrades in the thrones of the cities he had conquered.

But still, danger threatened . . . this time from the most distant east, from the very edge of Lemuria, where rose the frowning walls of Zaar the City of the Black Magicians.

Five years had passed since Thongor had faced one of the lordly magisters of the Black City, Adamancus of Zaar. The barbarian had destroyed the Black Magician with his own demon-wrested arts of sorcery, and rescued the princess from the grasp of the magician while his very tower was a seething chaos of magic flames. Thongor had come back across half a world to Patanga, and had promptly put the Black City from his mind, busy with the embassies of Zangabal, which had become the fifth city of the Empire, and with the thousand and one affairs of state.

But on this dark and moonless summer night, the dread name of Zaar came whispering into Thongor's dreams as he lay sleeping beside his princess. . . .

He frowned at the memory. It seemed that he rose through mists of dream to stand atop some mighty peak under a sky filled with a million blazing stars. And about the mountain's crest, as men will stand on council about a table, the cloudy dim figures of the gods loomed far above him, crowned with dazzling stars! Frozen with awe, the dream-self of Thongor had stood, naked and alone on the windswept mountain peak, with the shadowy and insubstantial visages of the Nineteen Gods frowning down at him—Father Gorm, the Lord of the Sky, with his winged brows and flowing beard and eyes of the fierce eagle; ancient Pnoth, God of Starry Wisdom, with the Book of Millions of Years clasped against his cloudy robes; smiling Tiandra, the Lady of Fortune, and Aslak the Smith of the Gods; radiant Aedir, the Lord of the Sun and his mate, Illana the Moon-Lady, and a shadowy host of others—and the Nineteen Gods spake to him in this fashion, amidst his dream:

"Beware, O Thongor, of the Black City, whose Eye rests upon all thy realm and thee. . . . Ponder the wise words of thy beloved comrade, Sharajsha the Great, whom thou knowest dwells now in our starry halls, and the warnings he didst write in that deep book of wisdom thou guardest . . . and return again unto the lands of the East, where thou mayest find the Crystals of Power, for in them doth lie the key to the future. . . . Beware, O Thongor, for a storm is rising in the East and all thy lands of the West may fall beneath the shadow thereof and founder, unless thou hast tamed the lightnings of heaven . . ."

And it seemed in his dream that Thongor had lifted his arms to the tremendous and majestic face of Father Gorm, and spake, saying: *"Hai-yah!* Thou Father of the Gods, ready am I to do what a mortal may in the face of the Dark

13

Powers . . . nor do I cringe from Danger, for he and I be comrades from of old, and oft have we measured swords the one against the other! But speak! Give me knowledge of this peril that impends, and lend me the aid of thy mighty strength against these enemies of gods and men!"

And to him the God made this reply: "*Know, O Thongor, that the gods are of a higher sphere than the world of men, nor may we do aught within thy world, under that Law that governs even us (for thy gods are but servants unto Higher Gods unknown!)—Nay! We work only through the hands of men. Such men as thee, cornerstones and makers of thy age, we influence through dreams and portents, visions and omens . . . for only in moments of ultimate peril to the universe may we take action in the world of men . . . therefore, be thou warned, O Thongor, and—beware!*"

The faces of the gods were of a sudden wrapped in swirling vapor. Clouds hid them, then rolled away, revealing empty sky which rolled and echoed with the thunder of stormy wings. Then the mountaintop vanished, and Thongor fell through leagues of whirling mist . . . down . . . down . . . to awaken bolt upright, shaken with awe, in his own bed. Beyond the window, he heard the guard cry the hour of three. . . .

Thus had he risen from his bed to steal by secret ways unto this unknown cavern-world below the great city. For here, in this place known but to him alone, lay concealed the magical treasures of Patanga—and now he stood before the hidden door of the treasure crypt!

With one hand he reached out and pressed the wall of rough rock. Stone grated against stone, and a massive slab of solid rock sank from sight, revealing a hidden room.

Within, hewn out of flinty stone, was a cubicle, empty save for a mammoth block of polished black marble. Atop this glassy cube lay an armlet of heavy gold set with a curious jewel, a rare chandral flecked with tawny, amberous fires.

Beside it lay a gigantic book half the height of a man. This was the Grimoire of Sharajsha the Great wherein the mage had inscribed with fiery metallic inks on thin sheets of metal foil the secrets of his magic arts and the fruits of his wisdom. Portentous and huge was this tome, bound in scaled green leather of tanned dragonhide, and locked with seven mighty locks of steel. Behind the black marble cube, clamped against the stone walls with brackets of iron, a fabulous sword blazed and flashed in the emerald light—— the matchless Sword of the Gods itself, which Thongor had wielded seven years before when his weird quest had led him to the Black Citadel of the Dragon Kings.

Never again would Thongor lift that enchanted blade, but one that was to come after him would, in the fullness of time and in the Last Days of Lemuria, employ the frightful powers of the Sword of Swords against the tides of Chaos and Old Night. . . .

Drawing a ring of keys from his pocket-pouch, Thongor opened the seven locks of steel one by one. And then he bent over the mighty Grimoire, slowly turning the glittering metallic leaves, as he read, and thought, and pondered.

Long did he ponder the words of the old wizard. The east was crimson with dawn ere he turned away and sealed again that secret cavern of treasure, and reascended the spiral stair.

CHAPTER 2

HARNESSING A THUNDERBOLT

The Wizard warned of evil Zaar,
And in weird prophecy foretells
A jewel-weapon, like a star,
Wherein the force of lightning dwells.

—*Thongor's Saga,* XVII, 4.

North of Patanga's central plaza, a small square called the Forum of Numidon lies near the River Gate. Thereon stands a tall house of yellow stone with a roof of red tiles, the home of Iothondus of Kathool, a young philosopher and student of nature. And thither with midmorning rode Thongor the king and a party of his nobles.

Long had he pondered the deep words of the old book,

15

and returning to the Palace of Sarks to share the morning meal with Sumia his mate and young Prince Tharth their son, now six years old, he was now ridden forth to consult with the youthful sage. In his dream or vision of the previous night, the gods had spoken of "the Crystals of Power." Thongor was reminded of that time five years before when he had fought and ventured on the Rmoahal plains of the remotest East. He recalled the shaman Tengri and his enchanter's staff, tipped with a glowing gem whose merest touch drained the strength from a man's body with a numbing shock. This mystery gem he had cut from the shaman's rod and fetched back to Patanga as a curiosity. The gem he had later given to Iothondus for study. And Iothondus had told him that among the Wise it was called a *sithurl* . . . a power-crystal.

Thus did he ride forth with mid-morn, to see if the keen wits and broad lore of the young philosopher could unravel this riddle of the gods. The sun stood near to the zenith; the day was bright and hot. Mounted on swift-pacing kroters, Thongor and his comrades left the palace grounds by the rear gate and took the avenue called The King's Way through the Old Town quarter to the forum. With Thongor rode that bull-chested old warrior, the Lord Mael; fat, red-faced old Baron Selverus; elegant young Prince Dru, the daotar or commander of the Patangan Archers, and Zad Komis and Thom Pervis, daotars of the Black Dragons and the Air Guard.

Apprised of Thongor's coming by a messenger, the sage met them at the gates of his house and greeted them as they dismounted, and led them within. Like all Lemurian houses in the Nine Cities of the West, his house was built in an open square about an atrium, or inner courtyard, which served as his place of study and a laboratory for his experiments wherewith he sought to delve deep into the secrets of nature.

His atrium was cool and shady, with striped canvas awnings as a shield to ward off the noontide sun. Long low iron tables with slabs of marble for tops stood about the walls, and thereon were set the implements of his researches, aludels and curcubits, crucibles and retorts and curious vessels of glass wherein strange fluids bubbled and seethed. Here and there stood massive athanors and wooden racks

16

of books and papers. In one corner stood the skeleton of a man articulated with copper wire; on a porcelain bench, a human brain floated in a bath of clouded liquid.

That bluff and hearty old warrior, the Lord Mael, peered with distaste at the crowded shelves and cluttered tables: a man of war, he gave his trust only to his sword and his king, and liked not those matters of the intellect which savored to him of witchery and the evil arts.

His old companion, fat, red-faced Baron Selverus, waddled into the court, grumbling and snorting through his fierce bandit mustachios, bending a suspicious eye on the tall and massive athanors, or wizard's furnaces, and the other paraphernalia of study. But the third peer of the realm, slim, dapper, foppish young Prince Dru, Sumia's cousin, glanced with lively curiosity at the apparatus and riffled with interest through the old vellum-bound tomes and the parchments scrawled with uncouth hieroglyphics that littered the tables and the crowded shelves.

As for Zad Komis and Thom Pervis, they stood attentively while the quiet-voiced young sage spoke briefly with the king. Zad Komis, daotar of Thongor's own veteran corps of hand-picked, seasoned warriors, the Black Dragons, had the silver-shot black hair and close-clipped grizzled beard of age, with the hard straight body of youth. In the glistening black leather harness of the Dragons, his great black cape thrust back over his lean shoulders, his bare brown body was that of a matchless fighting man.

Thom Pervis, daotar of the Air Guard, was stern and majestic as a stalking panther, keen-eyed and grey-maned, clad in the silver gilt harness of the aerial navy, with sparkling silver helm and voluminous blue cloak.

The young philosopher gained their attention.

"*Belarba,* sire, and my lords," he welcomed them with the familiar Lemurian word of greeting. "I have long devoted study to the crystal and am ready to demonstrate its weird secrets, as the Sark-of-Sarks has desired of me."

Iothondus drew from a locked cabinet the sithurl and set it upon a marble-topped table, together with certain objects. The power crystal was a gem about the size of a young boy's fist. It was cut into flat facets and pierced through the axis with a narrow filament of copper which protruded from either face in two odd nodules which a

17

person of our own later age might have recognized as electrodes. The crystal was dim and clouded, but within its heart a coiling mist of glittering sparks flickered eerily with flakes of green and silver fire. Mael and Baron Selverus regarded it uneasily, but the others closely examined the sithurl with great interest.

Iothondus, a quiet-faced, low-voiced young man, modest and sober of mien, clad in a robe of neutral gray, looked down at his glittering toy somberly.

"This much have I learned," he said softly. "The sithurl, which is found only amidst the trackless plains of the distant east where the great warrior clans of the Rmoahal nomads wander and rule, has a property unknown to any other substance in all of Nature. Alone, this crystal absorbs and stores within it the light of the sun. This the sithurl draws in and filters through its crystalline structure, transmuting it into an energy akin to the fury of the lightning, and storing this new force between the planes of its structure. I cannot say how the heat of the sun is changed into the tingling force of the thunderbolt, but thus it is. Perhaps it is even as the ancient philosopher of nature, wise Quonidus of Yb, said of old: *all energies are different forms of one primal force, heat, light, fire, and the levinbolts of heaven.*"

His low, thoughtful voice droned on, enumerating the rare properties and powers of the sithurl.

One of our modern age, could he have overheard this discussion, might have guessed that the power crystal was somewhat akin to the galena or corundum crystals used in the "crystal sets" popular in the early, experimental days of radio—heavy mineral crystals of lead sulphide whose unique quality is to permit an alternating current to pass freely in one direction only. Or perhaps the sithurls were similar in nature to an allotropic crystalline form of some photosensitive energy-absorbing metal such as selenium. The secret can no longer be discovered, nor the nature of the lost power crystals of the Lemurian Adepts determined with any accuracy. The last known true sithurl vanished from the knowledge of man in history's dawn with the destruction of Atlantis.

"The Sark-of-Sarks hath told me the tale of Jomdath of
18

the Jegga Nomads, who said that when the shaman's rod tipped with this crystal but touched his body he was paralyzed with a strange numbing force. The force is not strange: I have seen a ship's mast struck with lightning, and men caught in the nimbus of the thunderbolt were prostrated, numbed, rendered weak and helpless with the tingling force of the bolt. Thus it is with this sithurl. The force, released in a certain way, delivers a weak trickle of energy which paralyzes the nerves. Released in other ways, the results are more . . . *spectacular,*" the young philosopher said.

"How is this done?" Thongor inquired, peering at the mystic jewel with a curious gleam in his strange golden eyes.

"This metal rod which transfixes the crystal along the axis of its structure is the key to altering and controlling the flow of the forces stored within the crystal," he explained. "Also, the precise shape and number of the facets, as related to the plane of the crystalline structure, and the adjustments of these nodules, serve to influence the release of the forces locked within the sithurl."

The sage made a slight adjustment at the base of the metal bracket wherein the crystal was set, and placed it on one end of a long low table of porcelain which had been cleared of all other clutter. At the other end, he placed a wood vise, clamping upright therein a dagger with the steel blade pointing into the air.

"I have experimented with different settings, and learned how to release the inner forces at different intensities," he said.

Prince Dru eyed the apparatus dubiously. "You said the results could be 'spectacular'?"

The philosopher nodded. "Depending on the size of the crystal used, and the length of time it is exposed to the direct rays of the sun, the results can indeed be spectacular," he answered smiling. "Behold!"

He made one last adjustment—

KRAKKK!

A searing bolt of green-white fire clove the shadowy dimness with blinding brilliance. The stench of ozone assailed their nostrils. The dagger's blade glowed cherry

19

red—then fierce yellow—then sagged and folded to run over the top of the table in sizzling driblets of molten metal.

The solid steel blade was gone, leaving naught but a bent stub of blisteringly hot metal behind, standing in a cooling puddle of liquid steel.

Spectacular . . . indeed!

"Gorm!" Thongor growled, nape-hairs bristling with the barbarian's inborn dread of the supernatural.

"Witchery! Evil witchery," fat old Selverus boomed, and clutched the protective amulet of green paste which hung on a leathern thong about his red neck.

The others stared, frozen with astonishment, blinking against the after-images of that searing bolt.

"Or . . . *behold!*" the sage said, making another adjustment at the base of the astounding gem. Its greenish-silver inner radiance grew slowly brighter . . . a clear, soft, unearthly blaze of light that illuminated the awning-shaded court as brilliantly as a miniature sun!

"Heaven's lightning, and heaven's sun, combined in one magic gem," Zad Komis mused, rubbing his trim spade-beard thoughtfully.

Thongor recalled a scrap of prophetic lore he had read the night before from the mighty Grimoire of Sharajsha. He repeated it aloud. " '*The power of future ages lies locked in the crystals of the unknown East, the power to light the cities of man, or to crush them into dust. . . .*' "

Young Iothondus nodded.

The blazing radiance that glimmered like a halo about the sithurl waned . . . faded . . . and was gone.

"Thus it is, with this particular specimen," he commented. "Its capacity to retain in storage the sun's energies is very limited. A larger or purer crystal could emit a more powerful destructive bolt, or a steady illuminance that would last for hours. . . ." His voice grew dreamy, his scholar's pale face wistful. "There is now given unto us a tremendous secret, which can be used for man's good or for man's ill. With this wisdom, we could light the streets and the houses of our cities through the hours of darkness, that no man need fear the dark, the assassin in the shadows, the thief in the night. Or, by a simple adjustment of the faceting, a flow of sun-like heat, to stave off the cruel grip of icy winter . . . or. . . ."

"Or this power could be bent to the needs of war," Thom Pervis completed the philosopher's thought for him, in his deep thoughtful voice.

"Aye, my lord, there is that. And I fear that war shall be the first purpose to which we must employ the sithurl," Thongor growled, face grim. He had spoken to none of the warning the gods had delivered to him in his dreams the night before, not to his mate Sumia nor to these, the peers and commanders of his empire. But the words of Heaven lay like heavy stones in his mind.

He turned abruptly to the sage.

"You have found the key to releasing the forces locked with these power crystals," he said. "Would you know how to cut and cleave more of these crystals, to deliver stronger bolts of the lightning force? If we were to mount the sithurls in our airboats, could they blast objects from a greater distance?"

Iothondus nodded. "Aye, sire. Given crystals five or six times the size of this, my only specimen, I could cut them for that use in only days——"

"Then you shall have them, by Gorm! And should the dark wizards of Zaar strike against us, we shall defend ourselves with the very thunderbolts of heaven!"

"I would welcome the chance to experiment with new stones," said Iothondus, "and to explore the nature and potentials of this new force. All I need is a sizable quantity of new crystals. I can readily adapt them to distance-weapons, and I perceive a method by which I can affix them to tripod-mounts in the prow of the Air Guard's floaters and yet trigger their destructive bolts from the floaters' cabins."

Lord Mael cocked a mirthful eye at the quiet sage. "How now, my lad? A moment gone and you were bemoaning the use of the gems for warfare—now you are busy with plans for their use as weapons! How do you reconcile your ethics with the practical use of warriors?"

The philosopher smiled gently. "I am a student and a man of peace, no warrior. Yet am I wise enough, my lord, to know that a man can only practice the arts of peace and science in a realm powerful enough to defy and overcome

21

its enemies! In strength there is peace, and will ever be, until men are wise and noble as the very gods—which shall not be in our time, I fear! Hence is the profession of the warrior a proud and noble one, to be served and honored by those of us who may not bear the sword. Hence do I know that in such times, and in the world as it is, the needs of war must be served, if men of peace and philosophy such as I may be free to pursue our studies," said Iothondus who, although young in years, was among the wisest of the Wise in his mighty epoch.

Lord Mael beamed and swaggered to the sage's side, and clapped one beefy hand to his frail slim shoulder—a blow which staggered the smiling young man.

"Well said, my lad! Aye, and truthful words of wisdom, too—I like your spirit, boy!" Mael boomed heartily as the others grinned.

Thongor moodily stared at the glowing enigma of the small crystal . . . the tiny, insignificant bit of stone that was to change the face of the earth and alter the course of future ages. Then his mood turned, and the zest of adventure filled his veins like heady wine. To venture again into the unknown vastness of the eastern plains! To seize a mighty weapon for defense against grim-walled Zaar, within the very shadow of her ebon walls! His deep voice rang out like a trumpet, summoning men to war.

"Thom Pervis! Ready a score of your largest, most capacious airboats for immediate departure to the lands of the Jegga Horde. Place your most experienced pilots on the alert—we voyage east as soon as all can be prepared."

"Aye, Lord King!"

"And you, Zad Komis, command a picked company of the Black Dragons to stand by for boarding the fleet. Gorm alone knows what adventures and perils lie in wait for us as the world's edge!"

And thus it was begun . . . the Last Battle, wherein time and the gods should weigh the strength of Patanga against the evil science of Zaar, that one should fall, but the other—*rise!*

CHAPTER 3

SAILORS OF THE SKY

To guard the kingdom Thongor rules,
His fleet must venture to those lands
Wherein are found the magic jewels
And where the Druids' city stands.

As bright keels clove the morning air,
They soar aloft and speed away—
East, ever east, they flew—for there
The secrets of the Future lay!

—*Thongor's Saga*, XVII, 5-6.

Dawn burned crimson and gold in the east. A fresh salt breeze blew from the gulf, tugging at Thongor's vast cloak and stirring the gold-and-black banners along the roof's edge into life. Two days of busy preparation had passed, and the expedition into the unknown east was ready to depart. Dawn-light sparkled on the silvery hulls of the air-boats as they circled above the Palace of Sarks, awaiting Thongor.

On the rooftop landing-stage above the palace, the Valkarthan made his farewells to his princess and his son, the young prince. Young Tharth, or Thar, as they called him, was a sturdy, husky lad of six, tanned and lithe and sinewy, with the coarse black mane, scowling brows and strange golden eyes of his mighty sire. Thongor bent and scooped the boy up, tossing him into the air and catching him as the boy crowed with laughter—then handed him into the keeping of Lady Inneld and Lady Lulera, the two daughters of Lord Mael who served as handmaidens to Princess Sumia.

Then he turned and drew his lovely dark-eyed mate into the embrace of his brawny arms. He strained her against his chest, crushing her softness against his strength, and

23

gave her warm lips a resounding kiss that left her gasping breathlessly.

"Fear not for me," he said gently. "We but venture to the lands ruled by our friend Jomdath, the old chief of the Jegga Horde. We shall secure a load of the power crystals and return to Patanga straightway."

Sumia smiled and kissed him by way of answer. A warrior's mate in a barbaric age, she knew his life was set about with danger and peril. Although her woman's heart ached at the thought of letting the man she loved dare a thousand hazards half a world from her side, she said no word against his going. A brave man must do battle with his foes, or fall beneath them. She would have it no other way.

They clung together in a last embrace, and then he turned away to salute the others who had come to the rooftop landing-stage to make their farewells—Lord Mael and Baron Selverus, Prince Dru and Iothondus the philosopher, Zad Komis of the Black Dragons, in whose hands the command of the City of the Flame lay during Thongor's absence, and wise old Eodrym, Hierarch of the Temple of Nineteen Gods.

"*Hai—Thongor!*" they saluted him, and he lifted one powerful arm in a gesture of farewell. Then he turned to the center of the landing-stage, where his private airboat was tethered to a mooring mast. He climbed the rope ladder to the rear deck and bade the young pilot Falvoth Ptar, cast off the mooring lines. As the floater soared free and rose amid the other airboats of the expedition, he entered the floater's tiny cabin where a picked crew of his personal guard awaited him.

On his last expedition into the east, he had made close friends with the son of the old chief of the Jegga Nomads—the bold young warrior, Prince Shangoth, whom he had rescued from the grasp of Adamancus of Zaar. Shangoth had returned with Thongor to fight by his side in the Battle of Tsargol, together with several young Rmoahal warriors who had been among his most loyal friends and members of his princely retinue. These Nomads, Chundja and Jugrim and Rorik of the Axe, had stayed in Patanga with their prince to serve Thongor the Mighty. Now they accompanied him as he flew once again to the endless plains of the east where their brothers roamed and ruled and warred.

The domes and towers of Patanga slid away beneath the hurtling airboat's keel as its sharp rotor-blade bit into the fresh morning air. Thongor's personal yacht led the formation, with two lines of floaters falling off to the sides. The drumming rotors filled the dawn sky with their droning song and the green farmlands about Patanga whirled past far below. Soon they were beyond the Land of the Twin Rivers and hurtling swiftly through the skies above the wooded hills of Ptartha.

These weird flying ships were the key to Patanga's power, and the weapon which had given the City of the Flame supremacy over the other cities of the West. The secret of their flying power lay in the sparkling silvery metal that sheathed their slim, tapering hulls. *Urlium,* the mystery metal, was a magical alloy created by the strange knowledge of Oolim Phon, the Alchemist of Thurdis. Alone of all substances known to man, this magic metal possessed the eerie power to resist the gravitational attraction of the earth. The steel framework of the airboats, plated in sparkling urlium, was not drawn downward by its own weight. Instead, the pull of gravity was reversed and the craft would have fallen *up,* were they not cunningly counterweighted by the keel and ribs of heavy steel which balanced against the upwards pull, rendering the flying craft perfectly weightless. Powered by heavy springs which ran the length of the twenty-foot-long hulls, sharp-bladed rotors drove the aerial ships at a speed greater than a man could travel on kroter or zamph.

Oolim Phon, the old alchemist who had created the synthetic alloy, had constructed the first airboat. It was to have been the prototype of a mighty flying navy with which Phal Thurid, the Mad Sark of Thurdis, had planned to conquer the world. But seven years ago, Thongor, who had then served as a mercenary swordsman among the Guard of Thurdis, had been condemned to death in the arena for dueling with an officer. In his escape, Thongor had stolen the prototype airboat, and had used it later to defeat the legions of Phal Thurid and his power-mad commander, Hajash Tor, when they laid siege to Patanga. Since he wed Princess Sumia and became Sark of the City of Flame,

Thongor had built a mighty flying navy of his own with which to defend the Empire of the Five Cities.

Hours passed. The morning sun rose higher in the vault of heaven. When it stood at the noonward zenith, the fleet was over the land of Nianga. Here no cities stood. All was bleak and barren wilderness, a gray sere waste where few dwelt. All this realm had once been populous and fair, green with wooded hills and bright with glittering cities. But four thousand years had passed since that day when the God-Kings of Nianga had challenged the might of Heaven with their blasphemies, and the Nineteen Gods smote their realm with a mighty plague called The Curse of the Gray Fog. Since that terrible hour, no king had ruled in the drear wastes of Nianga, which men called The Gray Barrens and the Land of Death.

From their height, Thongor and his warriors could see the central lands of Lemuria spread out beneath them like a gigantic map. There to the north, from horizon to horizon, stretched the mighty range of the Mountains of Mommur that ran from west to east through the center of Lemuria like a mountainous spine. Far off amidst the mountains of the northeast, the noon sun glimmered faintly on the still waters of the Inner Sea where seven years before, Thongor and Sharajsha the Wizard had fought the Dragon Kings and brought their last stronghold down in flaming ruins.

Directly ahead rose the Mountains of Ardath, bulking purple with mist on the eastern horizon. And away to the south, beyond their view even at this height, the walled city of Tsargol stood on the shores of Yashengzeb Chun the Southern Sea. There ruled Thongor's comrade, Karm Karvus, whom the Red Archdruid, Yelim Pelorvis, had driven into exile and outlawry. Thongor had broken the might of the Red Druids who served the demon god, Slidith the Lord of Blood, and drove them out of Tsargol, restoring Prince Karm Karvus to his rightful throne. Today, Tsargol was the second greatest city of the empire and one of Thongor's staunchest and most powerful allies.

With midday they broke their fast with dried meat, figs, and dates from the Desert Country, the good black bread

26

of Pelorm on the gulf, jellied fruits from Tarakus, washed down with sarn-wine.

By evening, they crossed the River Ilth and flew above the easternmost of the cities of man, Darundabar and Dalakh, which rose on the shores of the great river, with seacoast Vozashpa far to the south cloaked in coming darkness.

Now they were in unknown country. Thongor had flown over these lands, but had never visited them. Even Shangoth, the chieftain of the far-ranging Nomads who rule the Eastern Plains, had never ventured into these lands. The trackless sands of the Desert Country lay below them now, where caravans from the merchant-cities dared the perils of sandstorm and thirst, among endless dunes of crimson sand wherein dwell the dreaded *cathgan,* or viper of the sands, and the most terrible creature of all the Desert Country, the fearful *slorg* . . . the woman-headed serpents.

The sun died on its funeral pyre in the west in a welter of crimson coals. Night spread purple wings across the continent of Lemuria as the fleet of airboats sped on through the gathering dusk. Soon the mists and clouds that veiled the evening sky were brushed away by many-winged Aarzoth the Windlord and his brother, Dyrm the Storm King. Stars blazed in jeweled splendor, forming a glittering train for the rising of Illana the Lady of Heaven. Ere long she rose in all her glory, the great golden moon of old Lemuria.

Young Falvoth Ptar, the pilot of Thongor's floater, wearied. While he napped on one of the bunks in the small cabin, Thongor took the controls and piloted the airboat through the night.

Ahead, hidden in the dark wings of night, the Ardath range ran south. Somewhere among its wilderness of peaks rose the great Black Mountain like a pyramid of ebon marble. Once Thongor had spent a desperate hour clinging to a ledge of the Black Mountain of Doom, marooned there during his pursuit of Zandar Zan, the Thief of Tsargol.

This night, however, the driving rotors of his sleek craft would carry Thongor and all his host of warriors far above the deadly mountains and into the empty and desolate eastern plains to which they formed a mighty wall-like rampart. Dawn would see them speeding above the jungle countries of the south, and with midday they would be

27

flying over the trackless lands of the Rmoahal, the Nomad warriors who were Thongor's friends. With the lengthening shadows of early afternoon, the fleet would reach the time-crumbled walls of the dead city of Althaar which, aeons ago, had been among the First Cities of Man. Today its broken ruins moldered among the scattered bones of the First Men who had raised it stone by stone . . . today, it was the camp and base of the Jegga Horde, and there Thongor would find his stout friend, the great chief Jomdath of the Jegga.

As Thongor's fleet hurtled through the night into the east, far away on the remotest southern tip of Lemuria, where the Black City of Magicians stood on the brink of a promontory washed about by the crashing waves of the Unknown Sea, an Eye watched their flight. An Eye of malignant darkness and strange evil, with all the unearthly might and power of Zaar behind it. . . .

CHAPTER 4

THE ALL-SEEING EYE

And all the while a Wizard's glass
In darkling Zaar where Evil reigns,
Kept watch as ship on ship did pass
In winging flight across the plains.

Thongor's Saga, XVII, 7.

The Green Eye watched!

In the midst of a vast domed hall of vitreous black stone was set a huge mirror of green quicksilver in a frame of shimmering copper. Set at intervals about this copper ring were great sithurls. The power crystals blazed with weird light. A tangle of copper wires coiled away from their electrodes. Strange forces seethed and tingled through the heavy shadowy air of the huge hall. Cyclopean walls of glassy black stone rose to a dome of crystal. No light burned in all that mighty womb of rock, save for a cone of shimmering emerald radiance that beat and throbbed above the pool of crystalline mercury—pulsed and beat like a Titan's heart, timed to the throbbing illumination of the glowing sithurls.

On a great throne of skulls, atop a nine-stepped dais of green marble, sat Mardanax, Lord of Zaar the City of Magicians. Mardanax—the Black Archdruid, High Priest of the Three Lords of Chaos.

Tall and gaunt of form was he, robed in voluminous folds of black velvet, his hands gloved in black stuff, his face masked in black and hidden from the sight of men beneath the cowl of his enveloping robes.

Through mask-slits, eyes of cold emerald fire stared down from the height of the Black Druid's skull throne . . . down into the swirling green and silvery depths of the All-Seeing Eye.

It lay at the foot of the dais, set into the black marble floor like a deep well, encircled with a rim of red copper. Within the circle of the Eye, that curious liquid metal, quicksilver, was held in the tension of unknown forces. Mysterious current flowed from the seven sithurls set in its frame, filling the roiling, swirling liquid metal with electric fire.

Now the seething pool of mercury grew calm. A sparkling mist of vaporized metal faded from the green mirror of its surface. Within the mirror's depths, a strange vision slowly took form, evolving out of chaos.

A vision of nighted foothills slumbering at the knees of great black mountains. Hills folded deep in purple shadow, their contours reflected dimly in black lakes that lay at the mountain-roots. Above, the night sky blazed with stars like fiery jewels cast from a careless hand on curtains of black velvet . . . and the great golden moon of old Lemuria set amidst the jeweled throng like a golden brooch.

Across the golden face of the moon darted strange shapes.

Sleek projectiles of glistening silver metal, wingless and slim, tapering to needle-prows. Low cabins rose from amidship, opening on rear decks bound in with an en-

29

circling rail. From masts that slanted out behind the stern keel, long banners flowed on the night wind—banners of cloth-of-gold, stamped with the grim Black Hawk of Valkarth.

The fleet of Thongor, hurtling over the heights of Ardath!

On and on the glistening ovoids sped, arrowing across the bright shield of the moon's mystic face. On into the east . . . and beneath his mask, the Lord of Black Magic smiled to see their strange flight. For the cold, cruel eyes of Mardanax of Zaar knew those bannerets of gold and black. They had gazed on the duplicate of those banners five years past, when the airboat of Thongor had burst the glassy walls of the Tower of Adamancus of Zaar, slaying the magician in the grasp of his own demons and setting free the Princess Sumia of Patanga and her defender, the mighty Rmoahal warrior, Shangoth of the Jegga Horde. Even then, five long years past, the cold cruel eyes of the Black Druid had peered into the whirling depths of his All-Seeing Eye to watch the valor and might of Thongor the Barbarian bring death and destruction to the great magician Adamancus and all his works.

And now, the Warrior-King of Patanga had ventured again into the unknown East . . . to dare the wrath of Zaar the Black City and the terrible vengeance of Mardanax, its King!

Cold eyes narrowed behind his black mask, the Lord of the Magicians stared into the swirling depths of his magical mirror and watched the fleet of Patanga as it flew over the endless leagues of mountain and desert, jungle and plain.

The Citadel of Mardanax crouched like a monster of stone on a hilltop that towered amidst the City of Zaar. About him, cloaked in the dark of night, the City of a Thousand Marvels slept, while on the cliff-like heights of his eyrie, the Lord of the City kept watch.

This was the seven thousand and fourteenth Year of the Kingdoms of Man. For seven thousand years the Black City had stood here on its promontory at the very edge of Lemuria, fronting the dark waters of the unknown deep. Aeons ago, the Nine Sons of Phondath the Firstborn had ruled here in the East. They and their sons and their sons'

30

sons had built the First Cities . . . immemorial Yb and vast Althaar, age-forgotten Nemedis the Father of Cities, and grim-walled Zaar of the South. During the long age of The Thousand Year War, the children of Nemedis and Zaar, of Althaar and Yb the City of the Worm had fought against the reptilian hordes of the Dragon Kings who dominated all the earth before Father Gorm kneaded the dust of the soil into the First Man and bled life into the veins of his creation from his own right wrist.

The Thousand Year War was over; the Age of the Dragon Kings was done; and the first of man's cities had fallen into decay and desolation, leaving the Empire of the East to fall beneath the thundering chariot wheels of the savage Rmoahal hordes.

All but Zaar. Still the descendants of her founders dwelt here at the edge of the world in the ancient city of black stone. For Zaar alone of the cities of men had betrayed the Heritage of the Firstborn: Zaar had leagued with the Dragon Kings, had drunk unearthly wisdom and dark lore from the cold minds of the serpent-men, and with their mastery of magic had learned to stave off the death of their city, shielding it behind magic forces like a mighty wall. Thus Zaar survived, at the terrible price of treason and betrayal to the very name of Man.

Oldest of Earth's cities, Zaar was coeval with Man himself. And these eastern lands where Man was born were already beginning to see the first signs of the great cataclysm in which Man's first home should perish. For already the stupendous volcanic forces which were at work deep in the cavernous heart of Lemuria had begun the remorseless destruction of the oldest continent. The promontory on which black-walled Zaar the City of Magicians stood was beginning to sink beneath the nameless sea . . . stark prelude to the Day of Doom, still hundreds of thousands of years in the unborn future, in which the entire continent should founder and go down beneath the measureless waters of the great Pacific.

As yet, Zaar staved off its destruction with a mighty sea wall which held back the immeasurable tons of watery death. But the Magicians of Zaar did not ignore the evidence of their own intelligence: already, and for many

31

years, they had been at work seeking a new home . . . in the remote West.

But the Magicians of Zaar were few in number, however, great were their powers of black magic. They could not overcome the Nine Cities of the West in open battle—or, at least, they did not dare to pit the power of their dark science against the valorous swords of Patanga and the other cities.

Instead, they worked darkly and in secret. For more than a hundred years, the agents of Zaar had been at work among the cities of the West, dividing them one from the other, rising barriers of jealousy, hatred and prejudice. So intensive had this work become in recent years that one of the Nine Wizards—the supreme Council of Magicians who ruled the dark city—had been sent in secret a decade before to redouble the work. This malignant being, known to men as Thalaba the Destroyer, had worked his way into the innermost confidence of Phal Thurid, the Mad Sark of Thurdis. It was Thalaba the Destroyer who had piled fuel on the fires of ambition that goaded Phal Thurid on to dreams of world-conquest . . . but the coming of Thongor had put an end to that part of the Great Plan. For on the very brink of victory, when the hosts of Shembis and Thurdis stood before the mighty gates of Patanga itself and lay siege to the City of the Flame, Thongor had come out of obscurity, a nameless and wandering barbarian from the trackless Northlands, to bring the banners of Thurdis down in defeat, to break the iron legions of Phal Thurid, and to trample both the Mad Sark and the scheming Thalaba of Zaar into the dust. . . .

But another phase of the Great Plan had been begun a generation before, when secret agents of the Black City had insinuated themselves into high places of power among two Druidical brotherhoods, the Yamath-Cult of Patanga and the Slidith-Cult of Tsargol. The Yellow Archdruid of Patanga and the Red Archdruid of Tsargol had worked hand in glove with the Black Archdruid of Zaar. Their evil cults had bred corruption and fear among the hearts of the men of the West. Eventually, both in Tsargol and in Patanga, these pilots had borne fruit: Vaspas Ptol, the Archdruid of Yamath, ruled from Patanga's throne, while

32

to the south, Yelim Pelorvis, the Archdruid of Slidith, held Tsargol in the palm of his hand.

But again—and yet again!—by some incredible miracle, this nameless barbarian, Thongor of Valkarth, had triumphed over the deepest plans of Zaar. Both brotherhoods had he smashed, slaughtering their leaders and driving the remnants of the two cults forth as homeless exiles, devoid of power and influence. Whereupon Thongor had bound the divided cities of the west together in his young empire, healing the wounds that breached them apart, welding them together into a mighty bulwark against the dark powers of the east.

This upstart adventurer, this Thongor, who was become the Sark-of-Sarks of the West, had built an empire then that now held five of the Nine Cities of the West together, where Zaar had hoped to have city divided and warring against city, until all were so weak that the black legions of Zaar could sweep down upon them and conquer the entire West at a single blow. Now that portion of the Great Plan, too, was ended.

These thoughts passed through the malignant brain of the Black Archdruid, Mardanax of Zaar, as he sat watching the flight of Thongor's airboats, hour upon hour through the silent hours of darkness.

Thongor of Patanga had dealt his plans crippling blows. Not the least of these had been the deaths of Thalaba the Destroyer and of Adamancus. Both of these were Great Mages of Darkness; both of these were Lords of the Council of Nine. And the Nine Wizards of Zaar formed a unit of mysterious purpose: in the Pattern of Chaos, they were irreplacable poles of power. With two of these poles gone, the Nine were reduced to Seven . . . and by that much was their power itself weakened.

Yet still the Seven of Zaar stood strong: Mardanax and Pytumathon, Xoth the Skull, Maldruth, Vual the Brain, Ramadondus Voth and Sarganeth of the Nuld. Even diminished by two, the power of the Council was surely strong enough to bring about the doom of the West!

When dawn reddened the mists of the east, the Lord of

Black Magic made an end to his watchful vigil. At his command, the weird forces of the sithurls ceased. The image faded from the whirling pool of molten quicksilver, and the throbbing cone of green illumination that beat above the sunken well of the Eye stilled its eerie pulsations. The green radiance faded from the vast echoing hall of black stone. The crimson of day glowed faintly from the crystal dome far above.

And Mardanax rose from his throne of skulls, tall and gaunt in his black robes. Step by step he descended the dais of nine steps. He crossed the hall to a distant alcove. Drawing aside the curtains of crimson velvet that shrouded the niche, he exposed to view a pedestal of lead upon which rested a weird sphere of metallic mesh.

Behind the black visor that hid his features, the emerald eyes of Mardanax closed. His magnificent mind concentrated its tremendous mental powers upon that sparkling mesh of radium wire that stood upon the column of dully-gleaming lead.

Magnified and focused by this instrument, his thought beamed through the City of Magicians, winging its strange message by invisible mental paths into the brains of his fellow mages.

One by one he summoned the greatest sorcerors of all the earth—Sarganeth of the Nuld, Ramadondus Voth, Vual the Brain, iron-thewed Maldruth, Xoth the Skull, Pytumathon—calling them from their dark tasks and grim studies . . . summoning them to a Council of the Nine Wizards . . . to encompass the doom of Thongor. . . . And in his secret heart, the Lord of the Magicians vowed that Thongor's doom would be more hideous and terrible than any mortal man had met since Time's First Dawn.

CHAPTER 5

HILLS OF THE THUNDER-CRYSTALS

From scarlet dawn to scarlet dawn,
They arrowed through the empty skies.
League after league they hurtled on,
To where the Hills of Thunder rise.

—Thongor's Saga, XVII, 8.

All night the silver fleet of Patanga arrowed through the star-gemmed heavens as they hurtled league after league into the distant lands of the unknown East.

Below their shining keels the land sped away, vanishing into the darkness far behind. Now they soared above the grim deserts of the south, where the age-old ruins of forgotten cities built in Time's First Dawn rear the crumbling columns of shattered palaces against the cold mockery of the ageless and undimming stars . . . then the towering ramparts of Ardath loomed up before them, crowned with that stupendous monolith of black marble men name The Mountain of Doom. They flashed above the clouded heights of the mountains and now the impenetrable tangle of the jungle country flashed below them, in whose darkly emerald depths the great jungle-dragons of old Lemuria battled screaming with the ferocious deodath and the kingly, black-maned vandar for supremacy. And then, as dawn flamed in the pallid east, they flew over the endless plains of the Blue Nomads . . . countless leagues of flatland and whispering grasses where the zulphar, the fierce Lemurian boar, and the untamed herds of zamph and bouphar grazed.

Aedir the Sungod drove his blazing chariot slowly up the azure vault of the sky and long hours were passed in rushing flight, but still the tireless engines strove and the keen-bladed rotors bit into the breeze of noon.

As the day waned and the shadows of afternoon began

to lengthen across the endless plains, a city arose on the horizon. Great cliff-like walls of gray stone, with looming towers beyond and the shadowy bulk of domes, came into view, and the silvery airboats slowed and dropped lower through the afternoon air.

Then they flew above the awesome ruins of the age-old city. However fair and strong the walls had looked when they uprose over the horizon, a closer view revealed them in all the horror of their pitiful decay. For the ages had dealt harshly with ancient Althaar and the remorseless erosion of seven hundred centuries had thrown down the proud city into a broken, weed-grown wilderness of crumbling stone. Where once a proud and mighty nation of Time's Dawn had risen and reigned, was now a stupendous ruin. Acre upon acre stretched the colossal wreckage. Towers reared but shattered stumps, or lay blocking whole avenues and boulevards with mountainous ruin. Domes riven beneath the weight of centuries had collapsed. Even the mighty walls in places had fallen, as if the earth had wearied with bearing up their weight after the passage of patient aeons, and had shaken their burden into hills of rubble.

Once, ages before, this city had been the home of a brilliant civilization. But today the stately palaces and hoary temples were given over to grim savages devoid of culture, a people without a past, whose lives were devoted to endless warfare against the cruel tyranny of nature and the brutal heritage that flamed within their own hearts.

For ages beyond numbering, the mighty Rmoahal warriors who ruled these lands had been a people dominated by weird superstition, doomed to lives of savage ignorance and unending strife. For this was the mighty and far-famed camp of the Jegga Horde, renowned in war. Life on the great eastern plains of Lemuria is one of almost constant and unceasing struggle for the rude necessities of life . . . of war against the monstrous beasts that roam the grasslands, and the equally monstrous men who share these eastern realms. For ages the history of the Jegga Nomads has been written in the scarlet inks of human blood. Here on the savage plains the hand of each man is set against the next in fierce and eternal competition for the needs of life.

Sometimes the Jegga warriors were locked in conflict with the mighty Zodak Horde who ruled the lands to the south under their dreaded war chief, Zarthon the Terrible. Other times, war season would find them battling against the lesser hordes of Shung and of Thad, or with the horde to the west, the Karzoona tribes. For the Jegga, like any other of the Five Nations of the Rmoahal, were wild nomads who roamed forever the endless plains of whispering grasslands in their gigantic chariot caravans, but rarely making camp in the ruined cities of the First Men, preferring the open sky whose faceless and unknown gods they worshipped.

But Thongor had come among them years before, to teach them something of a different way of life. The great chief of the horde, Jomdath of the Jegga, had been forced into exile by an ambitious, scheming shaman, together with the Prince Shangoth his son. The tribal elders of the horde, urged on by the spiteful and malignant shaman Tengri, had despised the old chief. Mighty warrior that he was, something of the gentler sentiments of civilization had somehow been born within his savage heart, and he had spoken out against the brutal fire-death and prolonged torture by which the shamans of the horde offered up their victims to the Sky-Gods. Thongor had saved the old chief and his son from a lingering and terrible death, and had overthrown the shaman, restoring the chieftainship to Jomdath and chastening the elders. Today, a new nation camped within the walls of ancient and immemorial Althaar, a people who no longer loathed and mocked the concepts of mercy and justice, kindness and love . . . a race which had at last taken the first great upward step on the stair that led from the red murk of bestial savagery towards the light of high civilization.

Below the airboats now lay the half-wrecked central square of the ancient city, and from the floater's cabin Thongor could see the mighty plumed warriors of the Jegga waving their huge spears in welcome from rooftop and wall and ruined tower. The fleet slowed, circled, and hung hovering, rotors idling, above the rubble-choked plaza.

A tremendous shout broke from a thousand cheering throats as Thongor clambered lithely down the rope ladder to the shattered pave, followed by Shangoth and Jugrim and Chundja and the other Jegga warriors of Thongor's guard.

Thongor came across the plaza, his great crimson cloak swelling on the breeze, to greet the old chief of the Jegga Horde and clasp his hand in comradeship.

"*Belarba,* O Thongor," the chieftain said, saluting his guest with kingly dignity. Thongor returned his salute, and stood aside as the fierce-eyed old warrior greeted his princely son whom he had not seen in long years. The restraint that is part of the natural dignity of the barbarian was visible in the simple greetings they exchanged. With searching eyes, the great war-chief studied every inch of his towering son from crown to heel.

"Hast thou borne thyself as a true Jegga warrior among the men of the West, O my son?" he demanded.

"Aye, my father," said Shangoth humbly. Jomdath of the Jegga snorted with evident disbelief.

"*Pfaugh!* I doubt not thou hast swilled down the fiery wines of the West and snored thyself into a drunken slumber like a besotted beast!" Jomdath spat, eyes blazing with pretended rage, as he sought to conceal the pride and tenderness that were all but overflowing in his mighty heart. "And hast thou still the strong arm of a true-born Son of the Sky-Gods, that canst battle untiringly in the service of thy lord, Thongor of the West? Perchance thou hast disgraced thy father's name in battle against the Lord Thonger's foes!"

Thongor restrained a smile. He stepped forward and laid one hand on Shangoth's massive shoulder as the warrior-prince stood with bowed head beneath his father's tirade.

"Thy son, O Lord of the Jegga, has in all ways comported himself as one worthy of his nation, and of his kingly sire," the Valkarthan said. "In war against the legions of Tsargol the Scarlet City didst his mighty ax engage my arch-foe, Hajash Tor of Thurdis, the Lord Commander of the armies of Tsargol, and with these eyes I saw thy son hew the head of Hajash Tor from his shoulders. Aye! and with that ax he cut a bloody path through the very heart of the host!"

"Hah!" Jomdath grunted. "Fairly done, but any puling babe of the Jegga——"

"And," Thongor pursued further, "with these very eyes I

38

saw thy stalwart son with a single backhanded stroke of that same great ax cut down three Tsargolian warriors and cleave asunder the pole to which was affixed the sacred war banner of the Scarlet City, toppling the proud standard into the dust at his feet."

"*Hai!*" A grin of fatherly pride split the stern and majestic mask of the old chief's face. "Didst thou see it, in very truth, O Thongor? Then, my son, art thou welcome to thy father's side, for I perceive that thou hast not been untrue to the name of Jegga!"

Grinning with inarticulate joy, Jomdath clasped the burly shoulders of his son in his arms, then turned, to shout at the gathered warriors.

"*Hai-yah!* O warriors of the Jegga! Give welcome to the great Lord of the West and all his warriors! And slay the beasts that thou hast penned, and bring forth ale and the skins of wine, and all manner of good things to eat. For, as the moon doth rise this very night, the Jegga Horde hold feast and festival in greeting to our friends who have come hither from the western edge of the world!"

"Hai-YAH! Thongor!" the warriors thundered, shaking their spears against the sunset sky.

When the great golden moon of old Lemuria lit the sky that evening, she peered down in astonishment at the mighty fires that blazed within the ruined plaza of the ancient city. There the lords of the Jegga Nomads feasted their guests and entertained them with war-dances and the thunder-music of the great sky drums. Whole bouphar-oxen were roasted in the huge fires, and sour ale and bitter beer and sweet wine flowed from a thousand wooden cups, while amidst the feasting, Thongor and his commander, Thom Pervis, discussed with the old chieftain the purpose for which they had ventured so far into the trackless plains of the distant East.

In truth, as he had hoped, Thongor learned that Jomdath knew of a range of hills that lay midway between the lands where the Jegga Nomads ruled and those on the southern marches of their realm that the dreaded Zodak Horde dominated—hills where the mysterious power crystals might be found. The Jegga warriors had no use for the weird gems, but knew they were to be found amidst the barren outcroppings of lead-bearing stone that filled the low hills. Often, Jomdath said, a far-wandering hunter or war-scout, taking refuge amidst the hills from storm, would see the terrific lightnings of the Sky-Gods drawn down to earth by the mystic power of the crystals.

And with the morning sun, a great expedition was launched from the broken gates of primal Althaar. While Thongor's fleet drifted overhead, Jomdath and Shangoth and a force of Jegga warriors rode forth to assist the Patangans in securing the gems they sought.

Thus it was that on the seventh day since the vision of the Nineteen Gods Who Rule The World came to him in his dream, Thongor rode forth with a mighty host of the Jegga for guide and escort.

Never before had the Valkarthan seen the Jegga warriors in all their panoply. And they made a fantastic and impressive spectacle of savage splendor, these nine-foot-tall blue-skinned giants in their richly wrought and ornamented leather trappings crusted with priceless gems and glittering and flashing with badges and insignia of rare metals! Their bald and towering heads crowned with nodding plumes, draped in fabulous cloaks of scarlet and emerald and saffron velvet stiff with embroidery of gold and silver wire, bearing in their massive hands the terrible Rmoahal war spears that measured fully twenty feet from iron-shod base to keen-bladed tip, they thundered over the grassy plains in a mighty caravan. Some were mounted on gigantic triceratops-like zamphs, in jewel-encrusted saddles of intricately-worked leather; others rode the thundering chariots of gleaming steel beneath whose ponderous weight the very earth shook. An honor guard of fully one hundred gorgeously caparisoned warriors rode forth with the Lord Jomdath and his son, to guide Thongor and the air fleet to the hills. And as he viewed the gorgeous spectacle in all its barbaric might and war-like splendor, Thongor's own savage heart thrilled at the primitive pageantry.

Ere long they reached the Hills of the Thunder-Crystals, and Thongor's warriors descended from the fleet to mine the coveted sithurls. This was an easy task, for the mysterious green crystals lay scattered about by the dozens, thinly buried beneath the soil or studding the mineral outcroppings of the low, rocky hills in jeweled clusters so loosely set they could be pried out with a sword-tip. Thongor bade his men select the largest and clearest stones, for from such Iothondus had said he could fashion the best weaponry.

Digging out the crystals was easy work, but the gems were heavy as lead and it proved sweaty and exhaustive labor loading them into the great airboats that were moored close to the plain to facilitate the task. But, as the sun ascended to the zenith and a noon-meal rest period was declared, nearly three hundred of the finest stones had been loaded aboard. For this, Thongor owed thanks to the proud warriors of the Jegga Horde, for their gigantic strength made easy work of hauling the heavy loads aboard the sagging floaters.

And then, as they sat in the shade of the flying craft to break the midday fast, disaster struck without warning.

Falvoth Ptar, the young warrior of the Air Guard who was pilot of Thongor's personal yacht, gagged suddenly on his food, went white of face, and fell slowly forward with a great black war-arrow quivering in his breast!

With a warning shout, Thongor sprang to his feet, tugging his sword from its scabbard with a rasp of singing steel. Cries of rage and terror, pain and alarm rose from the Patangans and the Jegga—a deadly whistling rain of black arrows fell amongst them, striking down men by the dozen—by the score!

The trumpets roared from the deck of the flagship, where Thom Pervis had mounted guard. Thongor's Black Dragons and the mighty Jegga warriors sprang to do battle—*but who was the unknown foe that struck without warning from the empty and desolate plain?* Search the landscape as he did, Thongor could see nothing! Save for themselves, the plains were empty!

CHAPTER 6

THE NINE WIZARDS OF ZAAR

And when the Lords of Terror learned
That he who foiled them in the past
Hath once more to their realm returned,
They plan a black revenge at last.

Met in their halls of ebon gloom,
The death of Thongor they decree;
And vow so terrible a doom,
None ever suffered as shall he!

—*Thongor's Saga*, XVII, 9-10.

The Lord Mardanax sat on a throne of black marble, his velvet robes drawn about him, his cold eyes gleaming venomously through the slits of his mask.

The great hall of the Council of the Nine was hewn from glistening ebon marble. Its walls formed a stupendous circle, and colossal columns rose along the curving wall to vanish in echoing gloom far overhead.

The throne of Mardanax the Lord of Zaar was one of nine great stone chairs that sat in a vast ring . . . and in the center of the Hall before the nine thrones, a mighty pit was sunken deep as a well into the marble floor. From this pit a sheet of crimson and golden flame roared up from hidden depths below, casting a shaking banner of red-gold radiance over the mighty chamber.

The other thrones were vacant. Then a dimness grew about the throne of purple malachite. It coalesced into a dense shadow which grew opaque, folding in upon itself, and became the figure of a man. The fountain of fire thundered upward, flooding the room with scarlet light, and from some unknown source, a mighty Voice spake slow and deep, filling the Hall of the Nine with clamoring echoes:

"The Lord Pytumathon, Prince of Magic, hath come!"

Immense was he, gross to the point of obscenity, his bloated paunch and flabby limbs clad in fantastic garments of purple velvet and lavender silks. Great gems flashed icy fire from his earlobes and the fat white fingers of his hands. He bowed once towards the black throne, and took his place on the purple. His face was one sagging mass of blubbery fat, bald as a babe, lacking even eyebrows, and his lashless pale eyes were like chips of ice amidst the sickly pallor of his visage.

Now from a hidden door a blue-skinned giant walked forward. A towering Rmoahal was he, his superb body clad in a distinctive harness of emerald-green leather and a huge cloak. His face was blank; his eyes shone dully, without the slightest gleam of intelligence. He stalked forward stiffly like a zombie, and cradled in his mighty-thewed arms he bore a loathsome, dwarfed and shrunken thing.

"The Lord Vual the Brain, Prince of Magic, hath come!" the great Voice intoned sepulchrally. The jet of scarlet fire revealed the pitiful and deformed creature that the blank-eyed slave carried up the steps and deposited on the mighty chair of green jade. Its shrunken body was no larger than a child's, but the *head*—the enormous, swollen, bulging head that swayed and lolled atop those narrow shoulders and that scrawny chest—was many times the size of a full-grown man's. By contrast, the face beneath that swelling, bloated brow was tiny, pinched, elfin, from which peered burning eyes of sharp black fire, like evil jewels.

The Brain nodded its huge, heavy, malformed head which wobbled atop a thin shrunken neck in a gesture of obeisance toward the black throne, and settled back in its huge seat of green jade while the Rmoahal slave took up his place behind the throne, mighty arms folded against his muscular chest, face blank and dead as wax.

Then in strode a magnificent warrior in scarlet satin and glittering steel mail, thewed and sinewed like a majestic tiger. Tall and stalwart was he, broad-shouldered and stern-faced, with mocking green cat-like eyes and strong lips which wore an ironic smile, framed in a short stiff spade-beard of black. A great sword hung at his side, and a vast cloak of scarlet satin swirled about his booted legs as he mounted another dais, bowed sardonically towards the

43

black place and sprawled with a gusty sigh in his great chair of sparkling crimson crystal. The fire roared up and the Voice spake like a trumpet.

"The Lord Maldruth, Prince of Magic, hath come!"

A dim haze of cold light grew into being about the fifth chair, a massive throne hewn from a single gigantic sapphire. It brightened—blazed!—and the Fifth Wizard appeared in a soundless flash of indigo radiance.

Tall and gaunt was he, fleshless as a withered mummy, his sere brown skin wrinkled and seamed with ages of unendurable existence. A huge enveloping robe of deep blue cloth shrouded his skeletal, stooped form, and as he thrust back the voluminous hood with one claw-like hand, his head gleamed bare as brown bone. The flesh had fallen from his cheeks, hollowing them. Beneath bald brows, deep-sunken in black-ringed sockets, his eyes burned with the sick fires of fanatacism. He bowed to the black chair and sat back wearily in his place, wetting thin lips with a narrow black tongue. And the Voice boomed forth:

"The Lord Xoth the Skull, Prince of Magic, hath come!"

Of a sudden the sixth throne of gray granite was occupied, but none could say whence had come the slim, small, quiet figure that had crept within it. His narrow face, bland, expressionless, his soft pale eyes and colorless hair, meek hands folded upon his breast, he was a pallid little man wrapped in close-fitting gowns of dim gray silk. He nodded quietly to the black seat.

"The Lord Sarganeth of the Nuld, Prince of Magic, hath come!" the Voice rang like a trumpet, filling the gloom-enshrouded vault above their heads with drumming echoes.

Six of the princely Lords of Magic had taken their places. But three stone chairs of the nine about the central well of fire were vacant. The seventh was that of Thalaba the Destroyer, that loathsome thing whose disease-crippled and fungus-eaten body had been destroyed years ago in the Battle of Patanga. The eighth belonged to Adamancus, that great Mage who had been consumed in the magic flames of his own creating when Thongor had demolished his tower. But the ninth throne? From his black seat, Mardanax demanded:

"Where is our brother, the Lord Ramadondus Voth, for

44

behold his seat of yellow stone lies vacant and empty!"

From the gray chair, pallid Sarganeth of the Nuld spake in low soft tones: "The Yellow One hath taken my place among the Winged Men of Zand, O Elder Brother. My labors there have gone well, but now that I have perverted the Nuld to our service, my task is completed and the Yellow One has assumed control of the final phase, for he is more adept than I in the mind sciences."

Maldruth spoke from the scarlet throne, his harsh tones sardonic: "Then soon shall the host of Flying Warriors descend upon Patanga the City of the Flame, to seize it by storm! *Hai,* Chaos—'twill be a joyous day! But what, O Purple One, of our secret ally within the very gates of Patanga? What of that vile and treasonous serpent the Patangans nourish within their very bosom, not knowing him to be an agent bidden to our purpose?"

The Lord Pytumathon heaved his gross bulk on the great throne and wheezed with coarse laughter.

"Our secret agent, the Lord Dalendus Vool, Baron of Tallan, is not as yet ready to strike and seize the throne of the City of the Flame, O brothers—but the time is soon! Dalendus Vool goes all unsuspected by Thongor and his lords, busily enlisting henchmen for his cause and laying his cunning plans towards that destined hour when the time is ripe to strike—when the Winged Warriors of the Nuld hurtle down on unsuspecting Patanga and invest her walls and guardposts, while from within, our ally Dalendus Vool hath seized the palace and the chief ones of the realm, making himself the master of the city."

Mardanax laughed.

"That time may come sooner than you think, Brother! We may not have to wait long years to taste the scarlet fruits of our vengeance after all!"

A ripple of tension ran through the hall of thrones, and heads turned to look at him as the Black Archdruid laughed with triumph.

"Yes, now let it be told, O my brothers! Our greatest foe, the savage, Thongor himself, lies within my open hand."

The metallic voice of Xoth the Skull came from the Azure Throne. "What mean you, O Elder Brother—how has this come about?"

And the Lord Mardanax recounted the sequence of events. He told how, with the eerie power of the All-Seeing Eye, he had observed the flight of Patangan sky-vessels approaching the borders of the East. Even now, he revealed, was Thongor and a host of his *chanthari,* his heroic warriors, landing in the ruin-choked central square of the dead city of Althaar. When he was done, Vual cackled with shrill laughter from the green dais.

"The fool!" the Brain said pipingly. "What madness possessed him to come within the reach of our power! And now———?"

"And now," Sarganeth purred in his colorless voice, "we have but to close our hand—and we have him in our grasp—eh?"

"Correct, Gray Brother." Mardanax smiled coldly.

The ironic voice of Maldruth broke the long interval of gloating silence that followed.

"And if he be in Althaar, among his friends of the Jegga Horde, how doth my Lord Mardanax propose to snatch him from the midst of ten thousand stalwart fighting men?"

"Easier than you might think, Scarlet Mocker!" the harsh cold voice of Mardanax grated. "For years beyond number, the great host of the Zodaki have fought and warred against the Jegga. And, know ye all full well, the mighty war chief of the Zodak Horde is Zarthon the Terrible, our ally who can sometimes be persuaded to perform small services for us. . . ."

Pytumathon wriggled his gross belly, chins and jowls quivering with coarse chuckles. He inched forward on the purple throne and his voice was thick with slobbering laughter as he wheezed: "And. thus, if I read your plan aright, Elder Brother, you will pit the Zodaki against the Jegga Nomads? *Hah*—a pretty spectacle for these tired old eyes! But what of this Thongor's flying ships, eh? Will not they take to the air and fight for the old man, Jomdath, and his clan? And if I remember, so potent are these flying boats that armed with but one of them, this Northlander pig defeated the combined hosts of the Two Cities, and the Black Hawk triumphed over the Dragon of Thurdis and the Silver Dolphin of Shembis—eh?"

"My plan is subtler than you suppose," Mardanax said coldly. "Nor have I told you all. Tomorrow, for some purpose I cannot read, Thongor and his men go forth onto the plains to a hilly region midway betwixt the lands of the Zodak and the Jegga Hordes. The Jegga will not be in force, only as an escort. And we shall communicate with the war chief Zarthon this night, and send him forth armed with our newest weapon, the Cloaks-That-May-Not-Be-Seen!"

The hiss of a sharply indrawn breath came from the Skull. His burning eyes glared with fanatic intensity and his gaunt form shivered within his enveloping blue robes.

"Ahhh . . . I see it now, Elder Brother." His dry, droning voice was harsh with anticipation. "The warriors of Zarthon will creep upon the escort unobserved, and seize this Thongor, hiding him from men's sight with a spare cloak ?"

"And bear him away from the midst of his fighting men, into the very camp of the Zodaki; and once they have him safely within the walls of immemorial Yb the City of the Worm, I shall be there to fetch him back to Zaar . . . where we may deal with him at our leisure."

A cold rustle of mocking laughter went whispering about the circle of the giant thrones.

"And now, my brothers, there remains only to decide the nature of the punishment we agree to inflict upon this *unza* of a Northlander barbarian," he concluded.

Then followed a debate between the Lords of Magic, wherein several gruesomely protracted techniques of torment were argued as to their respective merits. Throughout the discussion, the Black Archdruid sat back with a small cold smile on his thin lips. After a time he brought the dispute to an end.

"All of these methods are comparatively worthy, O my brothers, but none of them have quite that element of ultimate degradation it is our will to visit this Thongor of Valkarth. What is needed is to select the one particular punishment which is alone of all others, suited to match the enormity of the Valkarthan's iniquities against the Lords of Chaos, and we, the servants thereof."

Maldruth leaned forward from the scarlet seat. "Have

you a suggestion on this, Elder Brother?"

Mardanax chuckled gloatingly. "I have," he said.

Then, into the expectant hush that followed, he let fall one by one three enigmatic words. "*The Ultimate Sacrifice.*"

The cold words dropped one by one into the echoing silence.

Fat Pytumathon blanched, sweat gleaming wetly on his pasty, bloated jowls.

Vual's eyes snapped with black venom and his pinched thin lips parted in a leering smile.

Maldruth laughed ironically. But the others did not find the prospect humorous. Even the fleshless, withered body of gaunt Xoth quailed at the implications of this sentence of doom.

At length, fat wheezing Pytumathon spoke hoarsely from the throne of purple. "But, Elder Brother—no Magister of Zaar in thousands of years has dared perform this dread and awesome Ritual!"

The slitted eyes of Mardanax gleamed with emerald hellfires. "Then let us be the first to enact upon the Thongor of Valkarth the most terrible punishment conceivable to the human intelligence"—he paused, then pronounced the doom with gloating relish in his tones—"The Eternal Slavery of the Soul to Chaos!"

Then hooded lids veiled the unslaked fires of his gaze. He settled back in his great seat. "But these pleasantries are for another day. As for now, there is work to be done! I shall forth to the dead city of immemorial Yb to apprise the war chief Zarthon of the gladsome sport that lies ahead for him. You, my Lord Pytumathon, prepare a goodly supply of the cloaks. I must away to the City of the Worm ere moonrise."

The gross man in purple scratched one pendulous jowl dubiously. "I doubt if more than a dozen of the Cloaks can be energized in so short a time, Elder Brother," he wheezed.

"Very well, then; a dozen will have to serve," Mardanax snapped in cold, decisive tones. "Be about it."

One by one the Wizards of Zaar rose and saluted the Black Throne and turned to depart . . . each in his own manner . . . each to his own task . . . and each looked forward with gloating anticipation to the coming sacrifice, when the undying soul of Thongor the Mighty was to be delivered into the everlasting slavery of the Three Lords of Chaos.

The council was—ended.

CHAPTER 7

THE INVISIBLE ARMY

> And far amidst the barren plain
> Where rule the fierce Rmoahal,
> Death strikes in sudden scarlet rain,
> The men of Thongor cry and fall.
>
> A strange and terrifying scene—
> Death hurtling from the empty air!
> How can you ward off blows unseen,
> Or fight a foe—who is not there?
>
> —*Thongor's Saga*, XVII, 11-12.

"Gorm Almighty!"

The grim oath was torn from Thongor's lips as he lurched to his feet aghast at the sudden, mysterious attack!

A black arrow whistled past his shoulder—to bury itself to the feather in the throat of a mighty Rmoahal warrior. Another crashed against the glistening hull of the airboat at his back, and splintered to fragments.

He turned, sword in hand, bellowing for Thom Pervis. As he did so, a young warrior who happened to be standing at his side, a recent recruit to the Black Dragons, shouted hoarsely, "Lord—*beware!*" and threw himself before Thongor, shielding the Valkarthan's breast with a small light shield strapped to his forearm.

As Thongor froze, another arrow thudded home—to pierce half-through the round leathern *cherm,* as the small light buckler was called. Had not the youthful warrior extended his arm at that precise moment, the arrow would have sunk into Thongor's breast!

He glanced briefly at the young man's sweating face, and his strange gold eyes flashed with a smile.

"My thanks to you, Charn Thovis. But you are hurt——"

The young warrior shrugged. "The arrow has but slashed my arm, lord. No great matter." But blood poured from a long gash in the youth's forearm. Thongor's eyes flashed and he laid one hand on the boy's broad shoulder.

"You set yourself before me, so that the arrow might take your life and I might live," he said quietly. "Loyalty so selfless is rare, Charn Thovis. From this moment you are a *kojan,* a noble of the empire, and a captain of one hundred warriors."

The youth flushed scarlet with pleasure and began to stammer his thanks, but Thongor had no time to listen—he sprang to a ridge of the hills where Daotar Thom Pervis stood, searching the fields with keen eyes.

"I cannot see the foe, lord!" the older man said grimly. "Those arrows come from the empty air!"

Thongor gazed about. His men were drawn in a defensive circle, shielding their chests and faces with the light cherms strapped to their forearms. The weird black arrows fell about them like deadly rain. Nine bodies sprawled in gore upon the rocky earth and a party of the Jegga had ridden forth into the plain to do battle against the unseen enemy. Now they lay slain, bristling with black arrows, while their mounts prowled restlessly. It was uncanny!

The fierce old chief of the Jegga and his son, Prince Shangoth, had gained the safety of the afterdeck of the nearest floater, Thongor perceived. But from whence came this attack?

Thom Pervis ran one scarred hand through his gray mane. " 'Tis like an attack by ghosts from the Shadowlands . . . or as if the very air itself had grown arms and seized weapons to turn against us," he grumbled.

An arrow went hissing past his shoulder, and the old daotar ducked, cursing sulphurously.

"Put your helmet on your head, man. Don't stand there holding it in your hand," Thongor growled irritably. As Thom Pervis slipped the sparkling silver headpiece over his gray mane, the Valkarthan searched the nearby stretch of plain with keen, thoughtful eyes. Even his sharp vision could detect no slightest sign of their invisible assailants. It was, as the daotar had said, *uncanny*.

The wise thing would be to board the floaters and take to the air—they had loaded the fleet's cargo hold with some three hundred fine crystals before stopping work for the mid-day meal—but Thongor's warrior heart rebelled at the notion of fleeing from an enemy. Had he only himself to consider, he would have quit the shelter of the rocks and challenged the unknown foemen of the plain, to dare or die. But no longer was he but a single lone *chanthar* and free to wander the wide-wayed world with no higher duties than his honor as a fighting man. He had become a king, and must think first of the many thousands of his people who depended upon him. So, although it stuck in his craw to turn and run without striking a blow, he knew it must be done.

"*Gorm!* If we could only see the dogs, we could spit them with cold steel—or die trying—rather than hide here like yellow-gutted *unza* who dare not take the field and fight," he swore, growling with throttled rage.

"Aye, lord," the commander said grimly. "But 'tis no use! We cannot fight men we cannot see—curse the luck!"

Thongor growled grudging assent. "Well, one thing is certain—if we stay here much longer those invisible warriors will cut us down to the last man."

"Shall we try a sortie? Take them by surprise?" the older man suggested. Thongor chewed over the suggestion in silence . . . it was tempting, but he knew he dare not risk it. The one important consideration was to protect the supply of sithurls they had already taken. Those *must* be carried back to Patanga. It was no use wishing . . . he knew his duty, and no matter how bitterly he regretted it, he knew it must be done.

"No," he snapped. "Thom Pervis, get the men aboard the floaters. We'll cast off and get above the dogs where those arrows cannot reach. Then we can return to the dead city of Althaar in safety. Swiftly, now!"

"But—sire!" the old warrior protested.

Thongor cut him short with a curt word. "That's an order. Obey it! I don't like it any more than you do. But it's the only way. *Move!*"

51

Thom Pervis reluctantly signaled the bugler stationed aboard the flagship and shortly the trumpet-signal rang out. With admirable precision, the Black Dragons retreated step by step to the safety of the airboats, holding aloft their shields to protect each other as they clambered aboard the heavy-laden craft. Howling with helpless battle-fury, the surviving Jegga warriors of their escort joined them in seeking the safety of the flying ships, although they shook their mighty spears at the seemingly empty plain as they climbed over the deck rail.

Nearly all of the men were aboard now. Thongor and the Daotar of the Air Guard were among the last. They left the shelter of the rocky hill-crest and raced down the slope to the nearest ship. Black arrows whistled past them as they sprinted, thudding into the turf all about them like hail.

As it chanced, the old warrior was the first to gain the airboat's side. With an agility that belied his years, the commander put one hand on the low rail and vaulted over the side, cloak swirling. He knelt beneath a sheltering shield and stretched out his hand to assist his lord.

It was then that it happened.

Thongor halted, stumblingly, striking at empty air with his naked blade—lurched, as if he had run into something that the eye could not see—*and vanished from the sight of Thom Pervis!*

The old warrior gaped, jaw dropping in disbelief.

He could hear the sounds of a scuffle—panting, grunts, the thuds of blows—but could see nothing. While his napeskin prickled eerily, he saw portions of the dry grass flatten where Thongor had vanished—as if trodden by invisible feet.

"Sire! I come!" he shouted, and drew his steel, putting one hand on the rail to spring over it and regain the ground below. But now came other sounds—the thud and rustle of many feet pounding the earth!

From the empty air came Thongor's panting voice.

"*Back!* Back, you fool—take off at *once!* Don't try to rescue me—the rest of the dogs are coming—take to the air before you're boarded by men you cannot see!"

Thom Pervis groaned with anguish in his heart. Sweat beaded his face and dread knotted his throat so that he could hardly speak. "But—sire! My king!" he cried, torment making his voice break and quiver.

The panting, thudding scuffle came from further away now. Whatever had seized Thongor had dragged him some distance away—but in which direction, no one could exactly say.

Again Thongor's voice came from the empty air. This time it rang with the harsh cold iron of kingly command in it.

"I—command you—take the air—get—the crystals to Iothondus! Tell him to speed the weapons—mount them in your—ships!"

"*My lord!*"

"Then return—and seek me——"

"Lord! *Lord Thongor!*"

No answer came. The invisible voice was silent. Thongor the Lord of the West was gone, as if the earth had opened beneath his feet and swallowed him up in eternal darkness. The cold sweat ran down Thom Pervis' twisted face, mingling with tears, and agony seared his heart like a broiling iron.

The warrior beside him gasped and staggered. Blood blossomed from a sudden wound in his chest, and he pitched forward, flopping over the rail—dead.

The man who held the shield above Thom Pervis screamed as an invisible ax sheared into his arm. He lurched and fell, clutching the spouting wound. Thom Pervis, dazed, looked about him almost without comprehension.

The deck was being assaulted by invisible warriors!

Like a man awakening from a horrible dream, Thom Pervis rose stiffly to his feet. All about him sudden uproar exploded, as the Black Dragons felt cold steel rip into their flesh. Directly before Thom Pervis, a blur appeared on the polished urlium rail. Its mirror-bright surface clouded, as if a sweaty hand had clamped upon the rail. The deck lurched ever so slightly, as if a heavy weight was straddling the rail—the old daotar felt his bare arms roughen with the supernatural thrill of a premonition.

Like a blind man he struck wildly with his rapier at empty air. The sword swished through emptyness—and struck some unseen obstruction with bone-jarring impact. A hoarse booming cry sounded from the thin air directly in front of him and the deck quivered underfoot as if a heavy object had toppled from the side, making the weightless ship bob up slightly in the air.

The commander dropped a dazed glance to the sword he was holding. From hilt to point it was drenched in scarlet gore! It was almost as if when he had thrust the sword out before him, it had slashed through a man's throat. . . .

Thom Pervis whirled on his heel and sprang the length the deck, blue cloak floating out behind him like great wings. At the flag-mast that thrust out from the airboat's stern he swung up the rapier and brought it down with a vicious chopping motion. He cleft through the mooring line that held the flying vessel anchored to the tree. Instantly, like a gigantic balloon set adrift, the airboat floated a dozen yards above the earth.

The great voice of the daotar rose above the uproar like the thunderous roar of a brazen trumpet. "All craft—cut your mooring-lines and take the air—NOW!"

Like a flock of pigeons suddenly startled into flight, the Patangan fleet shot up into the atmosphere. The decks were crowded with struggling, cursing men who battled against things that could not be seen. But as of the moment Thom Pervis had hewn through the mooring-line, only a handful of the invisible enemy had managed to gain the decks of the floaters, and these few were swiftly slain and thrust over the side. Within a moment, the fleet was a hundred yards aloft and the men, panting with excitement and trembling with superstitions fears, stared down at the empty, tranquil scene below . . . barren rocky outcropping of low hills, with here and there a wandering zamph placidly cropping dry hummocks of grassy turf. That and the stretch of empty field, flecked here and there with an arrow-riddled corpse . . . but still nothing else could be seen! It was a living nightmare, but at last it was over, and they had escaped with the crystals, and with their lives—*Leaving the king behind.* . . .

The old commander's weary face grimaced at the memory of what he had been forced to do. He rubbed the back of his hands across his eyes, shaken. It had been the king's own command. And, as an old soldier, Thom Pervis knew a fighting-man does not question a command.

But in all his career of service, he had never obeyed a harder order than this. He felt . . . shamed. Broken. Like a

54

wounded thing, cut to the heart, he wanted to crawl away and be alone with his pain.

He stiffened, straightening his shoulders, clamping control over his wet, twisted face until it was harsh and cold as a mask of iron.

He was now in sole command. And a score of ships—a hundred brave men of the Air Guard and the Black Dragons—were his to care for. No time now to feel his grief, his pain: he must think and plan and pass orders. He must get the fleet back to Patanga intact. He must bear the load of crystals to Iothondus. Those things were the only matters he could concern himself with now.

There would be time enough, later, to mourn the dead.

And to *avenge!* His heart quickened. For Thongor's last command had been to see the new weapons installed, and then to return into the plains.

A cold smile creased his firm mouth. His eyes blazed with iced fires.

It would be a vengeance such as these barren plains had never seen since first the Hands of God molded them from the raw stuff of creation.

He turned to summon his bugler.

"Lad! Sound the signals as I give command. We shall return to the dead city of Althaar and let our friends of the Jegga return to their people—then at the greatest speed these boats can make—to Patanga! *Sound the trumpets!*"

On the deck of another floater, Shangoth crouched weeping at the rail, unseen by the others. He had watched with horror and fury in his great heart as Thongor had vanished, borne off by unseen hands from amidst his comrades.

In his hand, the prince of the Jegga clutched one of the black arrows that had rained over the decks from invisible bows. Only Shangoth had looked closely at the missile. It was unmistakably marked with tribal signs.

An arrow of the Zodak Horde . . . the hereditary enemies of his clan!

Shangoth had heard the last desperate commands Thongor had shouted, ere he had been overpowered by his viewless assailants to be carried off.

And Shangoth had seen the grief of Thom Pervis. And

he had watched the cold iron of command-responsibility enter the old warrior's soul and stiffen his spine to bear the burden. He knew that even were he to give this information to the Patangan chieftain, it would not swerve Thom Pervis from carrying out to the letter the commands he had received from his fallen king.

Shangoth knelt by the rail, crushing the arrow in his great hands.

Five years ago, when Thongor had saved him from a terrible death at the hands of Adamancus the Wizard of Zaar, Shangoth had laid his war ax at Thongor's feet—the primitive token of an oath of lifelong fealty that the warriors of his people took when they placed themselves in service to a mighty chief.

He had laid his heart there at Thongor's feet as well.

He knew there was only one thing to be done.

With the swift and simple directness of his barbaric kind, Shangoth swung silently over the rail and clutched the dangling rope ladder that trailed down through empty air below the ship. So sudden and unexpected had been the airboat's departure, that when they had taken off no one had yet remembered to draw up the rope ladder to its accustomed place when in flight—coiled upon the deck.

Now he swung down hand over hand, until he dangled from the last rung.

He let go and dropped, landing on the springy, spongy turf. The distance of the fall could have broken the legs of a lesser man. But Shangoth was a Jegga Nomad, with the iron strength and mighty thews of his proud people. Although shaken, he was unhurt. The tremendous muscles of his long and powerful legs had absorbed the impact unharmed.

He stood and watched as the fleet passed overhead and dwindled in the distance, hurtling through the early afternoon towards the distant walls of Althaar.

Then the prince turned and loped away at a steady, long-legged pace that ate up the distance—a pace that his endurance and stamina could keep up for hours, if necessary.

He knew the Zodaki camped in the ruins of immemorial Yb, the City of the Worm, many leagues to the south. He doubted not that for whatever purpose they had seized

56

Thongor, the Zodaki would bear their prize swiftly to the safety of their city. And Shangoth silently vowed to follow Thongor's captors, to seek him out somehow, even from the midst of ten thousand enemies.

Or die trying.

CHAPTER 8

CAPTIVE OF THE BLUE GIANTS

Made viewless by the Wizard's art,
The spectral foe—grim Zarthon's horde—
Seize Thongor from his men apart,
And bring him bound before their Lord.

—*Thongor's Saga*, XVII, 13.

Purple shadows of late afternoon were lengthening across the mighty plains before Thongor and his captors came within view of the walls of immemorial Yb the City of the Worm.

They had bound his arms with stout manacles of cold iron, clamping the cuffs and locking them on his wrists, with his arms behind his back. Once beyond sight of the Hills of the Thunder-Crystals, the invisible men had removed their peculiar cloaks, and whisked from Thongor the cloak which had concealed him from the view of Thom Pervis, Shangoth and the other warriors. And he saw them for Blue Nomads of a rival horde, although he could not read them for Zodaki from the jeweled badges that studded their ornamented, gold-encrusted leathern harnesses, as he knew not the tribal signs.

To the south of the hills, a herd of saddle-bearing zamphs had been tethered. The warriors bundled up the strange cloaks of slippery, glassy material which twisted the eyes painfully to look upon. They thrust the magical garments into saddle bags and bound Thongor with the chains while he stood grimly silent in his stoic way.

The cloaks, he saw, were more like hooded robes which

hid the entire body. Extra-long sleeves were folded under, concealing even the hands, and the cowl-like hoods were drawn down over the face. As far as he could gather from his brief experience with the mysterious swathings, a jewel-set brooch worn at the waist controlled the mystic power of invisibility. The central jewel, a huge *chandral,* a gold-orange gem of great rarity, which has vanished from the earth with the submergence of Lost Lemuria, seemed to be the control. It turned in its setting, like a vernier-dial that switches on a radio.

Thongor recalled, years and years ago, the great Wizard of Lemuria himself, the mighty Sharajsha, had given him a gold armlet set with a huge chandral, saying cryptically that the bauble might someday come in handy. And some time after receiving the gift, while a prisoner of the corpse-like men of the Lost City of Omm in the jungles of un-known Kovia, Thongor by accident had discovered the armlet to be a talisman of invisibility, which conferred the power of moving unseen to its wearer when the loose chan-dral was turned to a different position in its setting.

He also recalled that Sharajsha had been a magus of Zaar, long years and years before the mighty wizard had broken with the unscrupulous Black Druids and fled their city to take up his above in a subterranean palace hollowed from beneath the roots of the Mountains of Mommur in the distant West.

Thongor reached the conclusion that these magic cloaks of invisibility had been supplied to the Rmoahal warriors by his chief enemies, the Wizards of Zaar. It was an assumption based on slim evidence, but it seemed to make sense. For, since he had never had aught to do with men of this unknown horde, why else should they take this move against him—unless acting in the service of the Black Magicians?

Handling him roughly, the Zodaki thrust Thongor astride one of the zamphs, and they set out southwardly across the plains towards immemorial Yb. The zamph was a huge, strong and slow beast of burden that resembled a rhinoceros or a triceratops. Its hide was thick and leathery, a dull indigo in hue, changing to muddy yellow on the belly-plates. Its short, stumpy legs, hoofed with tough three-toed pads, could carry the beast without tiring for days on end. It had a horny, beaked snout like a parrot's, and horns spouted from between the small pig-like eyes and over the small tender ears. A huge concave shield of horn and bone protected its neck and shoulders, and looked like a natural saddle. In the Lands of the West, a zamph's raiders used this shield as a saddle, but the blue-skinned giants of the east, too large to use the horny shield for this purpose, strapped gigantic leather saddles atop the zamph's back, wherefrom they guided the slow-footed monsters in ponderous advance by means of reins affixed to small iron rings that pierced the zamph's pig-like, sensitive ears. Although a fearful and monstrously huge creature to look at, weighing up to three or four tons in adulthood, the zamph was actually a docile beast of vegetarian habits, easily tamed as a beast of burden, although somewhat slow-witted.

The party of Zodaki ambushers set off across the plains with Thongor amongst them, leaving behind a score of their comrades to harry the Patangans and their Jegga escort. The Zodaki who were left behind would follow later, once the floaters had escaped from their invisible attack.

They rode through the gates of the City of the Worm some hours later. His captors had said little to Thongor, nor had he sought to question them, but assumed the silent dignity that hid behind an impassive face a busy mind and searching eyes.

Thongor observed that the warriors whom he knew now to be of the Zodak Horde, were much more primitive and uncouth than his friends, the Jegga. Grim, ugly warriors, their savage faces seamed with ritual scars, they seldom laughed or jested with each other. Indeed, each Zodaki seemed to regard his fellows with suspicion and hatred. Silent and sullen, they only spoke to growl an insult or utter a brutal warning. Savage tempers flared out constantly—each Zodaki seemed perpetually on the brink of mutiny—and during the long trip across the plains, several fights broke out. A warrior, accidentally jostled or crowded by a comrade, would explode without warning into berserk fury. The expedition would then pause briefly, while two howling giants hurled upon each other, hacking with huge axes of bronze in an explosion of maniacal frenzy that left one or the other opponent a hacked and gore-splashed corpse. During these duels, the others made not the slightest attempt to interfere or to halt the fight. The others simply gathered about to watch, laughing with coarse amusement as one of their fellows went down under the flailing blade of the thirty-pound axes. The victor would then strip the fallen corpse of its ornaments and gems, and they would all ride away, leaving the cadaver for the scavengers of the plain.

From such exhibitions of brutal and murderous fury, Thongor gathered that the Zodaki were on a much lower scale of civilization than the Jegga warriors, their rival horde to the north. For although the Jegga Nomads were also sunk in savagery, a rigid code of challenge and acceptance governed their quarrels, and a strict dueling code was adhered to, with a neutral umpire to oversee each individual conflict, to make certain it was an even contest, fought and won fairly. Moreover, among the Jegga, duels were forbidden during military actions such as this ambush party. Thongor wondered how the Zodaki kept any form of discipline over their ranks during war-season.

When they entered the city, still more evidence was visible that these were barbaric and brutalized people who had gained only the lowest rung of social organization. Women were held in common among the warriors of the Zodak Horde, and children were ignored, mistreated, cuffed aside until such time as they grew to adulthood and could defend themselves, whereupon they were grudgingly accepted as warriors of equal status to the other adults of the tribe.

As they rode slowly through the ruin-choked streets, Thongor saw neglect and filth on every side. The Zodaki homes were hovels of inconceivable squalor, heaped with fetid garbage and devoid of physical comforts—mere camping-places, not homes. The Zodak warriors seemed to own no possessions save the gems and ornaments they wore on their person. It was as if they had not yet achieved a level of civilized organization sufficient for the concept of privacy and individual possession to become possible. Seemingly, one could not own anything he could not carry with him and be ready to defend at all times.

The camp of the great war chief was in the central plaza

of the ruined city. A fallen tower blocked off more than half of the paved square, and from a broken section of collapsed rubble, a rude cavernous space had been hollowed out to form the chamber of Zarthon's court. The entrance was shielded from the elements by a tattered and filthy awning hoisted up with two tall tent-poles. When Thongor came nearer, he saw this was the ruin of what had once been a gorgeous tapestry of the noblest art, now terribly stained and discolored but still magnificent even in decay.

Before this entrance, the ambush party halted and swung down from the saddles, dragging Thongor to the filthy pave with a brutal grip on his arm. He staggered to his feet, grim-faced and silent, making no complaint. They laughed coarsely at his impassive mask-like visage, and the taller of his captors, a brute whom the other warriors had regarded as the leader of the expedition and whom Thongor had heard addressed by the name of Hoshka, thrust a massive hand into the small of Thongor's back and sent the Valkarthan stumbling helplessly ahead of him into the shadow of the entrance.

The lair of Zarthon was a hovel of indescribable filth that reeked with an effluvia of decay which struck the nostrils like a blow. All about the cluttered chamber lay the spoils of conquest, the loot of the lesser hordes. Caskets burst open, spilling forth glittering pools of gemmy fire. Vases and statuettes of gold and silver, jazite and electrum, were tumbled underfoot, amongst the garbage of rotting food, smeared fruit, spilt wine and gnawed meat-bones.

In the center of the chamber was a raised platform which bore an ivory throne-like chair of exquisite design and carving, much stained with filth and droppings. Upon this kingly seat squatted the most hideous and repugnant beast in human form that Thongor had ever seen. His bloated and enormous body, bulging with monstrous, over-developed muscles almost to the point of deformity, was gross and obscene in its nakedness. Hung upon this loathsome carcass was an incredible wealth of jeweled ornaments. His gorgeous trappings were literally crusted with blazing gems, and belts and straps which crisscrossed his bull-like torso in a complex harness were sewn thickly with coin-like plates of red gold. The fantastic girdle which restrained his gross paunch was one dazzling mass of solid diamonds and supported a small armory of jewel-encrusted daggers and dirks, a huge scimitar and a mighty axe of bronze with a handle of gold set with huge uncut rubies.

The jeweled wealth that flashed and blazed from his ornaments could not, however, detract from the hideousness of his appearance. His huge bald head was stamped with all the signs of cruelty and lust a human visage could contain. The iron strength and warlike manhood of the mighty chief were debased and soiled by the marks of debauchery that showed in the loose wet lips and the rings of puffy fat that circled his small, cold eyes, the whites whereof were bloodshot from the aftermath of some gluttonous appetite of the animal passions.

No single sign of kingly or even manly dignity and pride could be ascertained in all his gross, sprawling bulk. From some disease or accident, his dangling mouth loosed a continuous dribble of spittle which drooled upon the massive, corded breast. The lineaments of cruelty and bestial cunning were cut deeply on his unspeakable face. Fang-like and yellowing tusks thrust from his underslung jaw to twist his upper lip into a perpetual sneer. In one filthy paw, which glittered with jewels, he held a winecup of enormous size, from which he drank noisily as Thongor stumbled before the throne. In the other, he clutched a greasy leg of half-raw beef over which he gnawed and slobbered between gulps of wine, cold little pig-eyes moving over Thongor as he sated his belly.

"So this is the little *unza* the Lords of Zaar bade us snare, eh?" he growled. The warriors who lolled about the dais made loud, obsequious laughter at the coarse jest, for an unza is a Lemurian rodent whose repulsive eating-habits, combined with a noted cowardice, make its name a favored epithet.

"Aye, Magnificent One!" the brutal Hoshka said, fawningly. He knelt and lay before the feet of Zarthon the Valkarthan broadsword he had taken from his captive. Its keen gray steel gleamed cleanly amidst the foul mingling of splendor and filth.

Thongor made no utterance, but his stern majestic stance, proud and unyielding, spoke for him, and his fierce golden eyes were eloquent of contempt and disdain.

62

Irked at the captive's silence, Zarthon tossed his wine-cup clanking aside on the garbage-littered floor, and leaned forward.

"Speak, little one—you are among warriors here! Why should the mighty one of the Black City go to such lengths to seize a puny youngling like you? Have you something they want?" A flash of greed shone momentarily in Zarthon's cold little eyes. He belched, wiped one greasy paw across an equally greasy mouth. Then, when Thongor made no reply, he flung the leg of dripping meat full in the Valkarthan's face and roared with phlegmy laughter as the unexpected blow made Thongor stagger.

He wiped his hand over his naked thigh, and reached out.

"Hoshka—hand me the outlander's steel," the war chief demanded.

A deep-throated growl of warning rumbled from Thongor's chest. His gold eyes blazed tiger-like. Among his people, no man handles another's weapon, for a man's sword, like his mate, is a matter of personal honor.

Zarthon paid no heed to the low growl. He would have been wiser had he done so. For behind his back, Thongor's great wrists were straining and cables of bronze sinew were rising and writhing along his powerful back and shoulders.

Once before he had been chained by the Nomads of the East, when rebellious members of the Jegga Horde sought to burn the old chief, Jomdath, and his Valkarthan friend at the fire-stake. Thongor had discovered at that time that the manacles the Nomads used to fasten his wrists were fashioned for the huger limbs of the blue-skinned giants, and that it was possible to remove his from the gyves with effort. Now, unseen by the Zodak warriors, whose attention was bent on their lord, he sought to free himself in a similar manner. He succeeded, leaving a few square inches of raw skin behind.

The first thing that Zarthon knew of Thongor's escape was the impact of an iron fist that drove with the sickening force of a blacksmith's hammer into the pit of his stomach. Thongor had sprung upon the throned figure with the swift rush of a jungle cat. As Zarthon folded in pain, clutching his paunch and retching with nausea, Thongor snatched his sword from nerveless hands and swung swift as

63

lightning to bury the clean steel in the putrid heart of his brutish captor, Hoshka.

Uproar exploded about him—a score of howling savage warriors sprang to defend their lord, galvanized into berserk frenzy.

But Zarthon swept them aside with one mighty arm while he tore from his girdle the great scimitar and, recovering from the effects of Thongor's blow, swept the keen blade at the head of the puny wretch who had dared lay violent hands on his sacred person.

But when the blow landed, Thongor was not there to meet it. He ducked under the war chief's furious swing, and sank the point of his sword into Zarthon's beefy shoulder. With an inarticulate, slobbering screech of pain and fury, the wounded monarch let fall the weighty scimitar and hurled himself upon Thongor bare-handed to crush him in a bear-like embrace. But the Valkarthan nimbly dodged under the enraged Zodaki's arms and slashed him painfully in one naked thigh. Roaring with rage, the ten-foot colossus lurched as the wounded limb gave way beneath him, and staggered to recover his balance.

And Thongor struck him squarely on the point of his jaw. It was a terrific blow. Thongor's iron fist came up from the level of his knees, with all the steely strength of arm and back and shoulders behind it, to connect with staggering impact.

It was probably the first time in his long and terrible life that Zarthon of the Zodaki had been struck in the face.

He went over backwards and crashed from the edge of the dais atop a sprawling heap of his warriors. His contorted face, black with congested fury, was bruised and aching and swollen from the weight of Thongor's blow. But it was the indignity of the blow, the insult of it, the affront to his self-esteem that pained him the most. After a long, shuddering moment of shocked disbelief, of dazed vertigo, Zarthon went mad with frustrated rage. He staggered to his feet, shaking himself like a wounded bull, then turned on his men, feeling them to right and left with terrific blows of his ham-like paws. Seizing up a great ax, he turned to cleave Thongor into gobbets—but the lithe bronze figure of his taunting and elusive adversary had *vanished!*

Alone on the throne-platform in the center of the chamber, ringed about with ferocious enemies, Thongor had taken advantage of the momentary lapse in attention to him as the Zodaki rushed to aid their fallen, dazed chief. He crouched, powerful muscles coiling in his long sinewy legs, then sprang into the air, strong hands clamping a firm hold on the age-blackened wood of the rafter directly above the throne.

His keen, searching eyes had spotted a black opening in the further wall at the rear of the room. Now, swinging himself up and atop the rafter, he ran lightly along its length to the end of the chamber—swung lithely down and was through the further exit in a bronze blur of moving limbs. He was gone from sight almost before the bewildered Rmoahals noticed he was absent from the throne-platform.

But a sharp-eyed young warrior at the rear of the throng had spied his moving figure in flight, and raised the pack howling on his trail.

Beyond the black door, Thongor found himself in a narrow tunnel-like corridor between two broken walls of moldering masonry. This he raced down, knowing not where it might lead him, his great sword flashing in one capable fist. Like a pack of demons, the Zodaki poured through the rear entrance in close pursuit, led by the limping, lumbering bulk of their maddened war chief. The white foam of blind fury dribbled from Zarthon's howling, swollen jaws and his eyes raged with scarlet blood-lust.

At the end of the narrow corridor stood some sort of rude shrine to whatever devils of the pit the brutish Nomads worshipped. Behind the blood-spattered low altar yawned a black pit which fell down into the depths of the earth.

Thongor paused on its brink, gazing swiftly around. There was no other way he could go—and in a second the pack of berserk warriors would be upon him to pull him down like slavering hounds. Sword in hand, he sprang into the unknown depths below!

Zarthon and his warriors halted their mad rush at the edge of the well, and peered down into the black deeps beneath. Naught but a cold breeze rose from the pit, laden with an unholy reptilian stench of unspeakable foulness, like a monstrous den of serpents.

Into *this* had Thongor fallen. . . .

Zarthon stood looking down.

He smiled . . . a cold, mirthless grin of leering cruelty.

Then he began to *laugh*.

CHAPTER 9

The Jegga thunder into strife—
War-horns roar from brazen mouth!
To dare and die, for Thongor's life,
Against the Zodak of the south.

—*Thongor's Saga*, XVII, 14.

The scarlet banners of sunset were unfurled athwart the west as the mighty legions of the Jegga Horde streamed through the broken gates of the dead city of Althaar and poured across the grassy plains in a mailed and glittering flood of grim-faced warriors.

At the head rode Jomdath the old chief who had led them through a thousand battles to the bright gates of victory. Now he rode forth to the most portentous battle of his life . . . for in his savage heart, the fierce-eyed old Lord of the Jegga Nomads swore an oath that he would go up against the very walls of Yb and take them by storm, to spit the accursed, foul and stinking heart of Zarthon of the Zodaki on his steel, or perish in the attempt.

For Jomdath, as well as his son Prince Shangoth, had read the tribal markings on the terrible black arrows that had rained from the empty sky upon them there among the Hills of the Thunder-Crystals. And Jomdath knew it was his ancient foe, the age-old enemies of his people, the Zodak Horde to the South, who had so shamefully launched a cowardly attack on them from under the cover of some magic shield of invisibility.

It was they, the Zodaki, who had slain or stolen away the great Thongor from amidst the protective escort of the Jeg-

66

ga. And Jomdath swore grimly that this insult to the honor of his people would be washed away in blood ere the world was one day older. He vowed to render the proud escutcheon of his name stainless, or die trying.

Thus, no sooner had Thom Pervis and the Patangan fleet of airboats returned the chief and his surviving warriors to the safety of their camp in the ruined city of Althaar, and departed to bear the precious power crystals to Iothondus in Patanga, that the great war-horns of the Jegga Nomads had run to the welkin with the iron-throated call to war!

Now, as the dark wings of night stretched out to cover the sky and drown the earth beneath their inky shade, the mighty Jegga Horde thundered to war.

The grassy plains shook beneath the ponderous tread of the great zamphs who bore on their broad backs ten thousand mailed warriors with plumed crests and towering spears. The earth groaned beneath the grinding weight of the great, broad-wheeled metal war chariots of the Jegga warriors as they thundered into the wilderness of the endless plains beneath a black sky blazing with a million stars that peered down like curious eyes upon this mighty spectacle of barbaric savagery.

Without rest or pause the horde advanced across the measureless grasslands through the inky blackness of the night. But when, hours later, the great golden moon of old Lemuria rose beyond the edge of the world to flood the plains with her silken, shimmering radiance, she looked upon a fantastic scene.

For the Jegga Horde reached, by the hour of moonrise, the ruined walls of elder and immemorial Yb the City of the Worm. Gilded with the glorious moonlight, the broken walls and riven domes, the crumbling facades of the ancient palaces with their fallen columns and black, empty windows like the eye-sockets of a skull, the streets and squares littered with rubble and overgrown with centuries of unchecked weedy growth, looked for all the world like some fantastic and forgotten city sunken in reed-grown ruin beneath a golden sea.

Great fires roared in the streets, and a clamorous thunder arose from shouting thousands, as the Jegga Horde drew up in all their glittering war panoply before the breached and fallen walls. But not a single watchman stood to his post on the walls, and not a single Zodaki saw the arrival of their hereditary foemen. For the entire city was roiling in drunken fury over the escape of Thongor and the indignities he had wrought upon their dreaded chief.

Zarthon himself, his bleeding wounds carelessly bound in strips of torn cloth ripped from a cloak, was roaring drunk, having imbibed deeply from the sour sarn-wine his people brewed. He had swilled down the potent fluid to salve the internal injuries done to his pride and sense of self-importance, rather than to numb and dull the ache of his poorly tended wounds. And to calm and cool his furious temper. For no sooner had Thongor escaped into the black cavern beneath the dead city of Yb, than Zarthon had turned on those who had been by his side when the bold Valkarthan escaped, and cut down a half-dozen of them in the unbridled fury of his anger. That *he*, the mightiest and most feared conqueror on earth, could be insulted, struck down and made to look a fool while a roomful of his most savage warriors stood by idle, gaping and slack-jawed as awe-struck girl-children, was a goad that stung his vile temper to berserk fury.

Thus, while the rest of the horde came running, Zarthon had run amok, turning upon his men like a blood-maddened tiger, striking about him with blind, drunken fury. And now the whole populace of the city quailed and shrank before his roaring, foul-mouthed curses, as steeped in potent liquor, he lurched and staggered about the central plaza, striking at frightened men at blind random, and leaving their screaming corpses to flop and wriggle, ignored, behind him on the stone pave.

Silent as death, the warriors of the Jegga crept through the thousand places where the great walls of Yb had fallen through neglect or earthquake or internal decay.

Through the open and unguarded gates, the mighty chariots of Jomdath's host rumbled on creaking wheels that crunched and clanked noisily over fallen pavestones, but all the noise they made was drowned in the uproar from the central square where the drunken war chief raged and murdered, watched by a frightened and mutinous circle of his men.

A squeak of terror—a naked infant, a scrawny little boy, fled from the throng to escape the noise and confusion. Zarthon's inflamed eye spotted the awkward child, and with a terrible hoarse roar he swept out the glittering scimitar of steel whose shining curve was wet with hot and reeking gore and cut down the frightened lad with a fearful crunch of breaking bones.

Dead silence fell over the watching throng. Scarred hands in secret fondled sword-hilt and dagger-butt. Angry, rebellious eyes flamed with mute resentment. But naught occurred in the interval; in a moment, had one leader stepped forward to form an example behind which the mob could stampede, riot and fury could have exploded across the corpse-littered square, to sweep the broken body of the war chief to the scarlet gates of hell.

But nothing happened. In the tense and deadly hush, Zarthon spurned the broken body of the dead child with one limping foot, and laughed with long phlegmy peals of bloody mirth. Then his laugh was cut short.

As if by magic, a crimson arrow flashed into view, vibrating in his chest!

Zarthon lurched, staring at the thrumming shaft stupidly, eyes glazed and dull, mouth hanging slack and wet. The great scimitar dropped from one limp hand, ringing on the stony pave. He lifted one hand to pluck feebly, tearing the scarlet shaft from his flesh with a thick grunt of pain, flinging it from him.

It clattered on the tiles, and men looked at it wonderingly. In the endless wars that raged eternally between the Jegga and the Zodaki, and between them and the lesser hordes of the Shung, the Thad and the Karzoona, an arrow, clearly stamped with tribal markings and shot into the enemy city, was the equivalent of a declaration of war.

The scarlet shaft bore Jegga markings.

And then the world went mad!

Trumpets rang and war zamphs screamed like steam-whistles. The crowd that encircled Zarthon wavered—and broke! In a hurtling rush, the great war-chariots of the Jegga Horde rolled on thundering wheels through the milling throng, across the shrieking bodies of those whose feet were not agile enough to carry them from the path of the spike-wheeled and steel-shod juggernauts, and burst in-to the plaza.

From ten thousand throats, the war-cry of the Jegga

burst in an earth-shaking shout.

Scarlet arrows whistled through the air, to fall in a barbed and deadly rain upon the crowd.

And Zarthon stood stupidly, swaying on drunken feet, as one unable to comprehend the swift change in events.

The lead chariot rolled up to him, and the grim, stern, majestic figure of the old chief, Jomdath of the Jegga, stared down at him, bow in hand.

One numb paw went fumbling across his gem-studded girdle, and Zarthon searched dazedly for the scimitar that he had let fall moments before. Instead, his scarred fingers closed on the handle of his mighty bronze ax. He tore it loose and swung back his great corded arm to hurl it in the very face of Jomdath. But the Jegga chieftain raised the bow and loosed a second scarlet arrow. It blossomed from between Zarthon's scowling brows.

His great, ugly and misshapen face turned the dull leaden hue of cold ashes. His enflamed eyes went blank and dull. His tusked jaw gaped open in an idiot leer . . . and Zarthon slowly, like a ponderous collapsing tower whose foundations are shorn away by some cataclysmic blow, fell forward on his face, dead as the cold stone he befouled with his gore.

Now the square exploded into a fury of carnage. Struggling knots of men fought together in the drenching golden moonlight like demoniac monsters from some awful frieze. Time and again, the Zodaki gathered to lead a charge, but were swept with the withering rain of the scarlet arrows, and melted before their stinging, whistling blast like ice before a furnace's breath.

Chariots thundered through the streets, herding howling warriors before them into cul-de-sacs, slaughtering the Zodaki where they stood backed against stony walls.

Mounted on their great war zamphs, the triumphant Jegga warriors rode back and forth through riotous mobs of screaming, fleeing Zodaki, laying about them with glittering swords that soon left trails of scattering scarlet drops on the moonlit air. Many fell to crunch into bloody smears under the ponderous tread of the great zamphs. Others were caught in the brazen beaks of the zamphs, sheared in half by clamping powerful jaws.

One by one, score by score, in their hundreds and their thousands, they died.

Never had the endless plains of the East seen so terrible a vengeance, so frightful a battle, as this that Jomdath of the Jegga waged upon the broken hordes of the Zodaki, in the streets and squares of the dead city amidst the measureless plain!

It did not end soon, but it did end at last. The crimson rays of dawn had struck to flame the upper stories of the palaces of immemorial Yb, when quiet at last reigned over the blood-soaked city.

In the fullness of their victory, the Jegga were not unmindful of the lessons Thongor of the West had taught them regarding the wisdom of justice, mercy and restraint.

Only the warriors of the Zodaki were hunted down and slain. And of the warriors, only those who refused to lay down their weapons and surrender.

The women and children, the aged and the crippled, the slaves and all the warriors wise enough to yield over their arms, were spared.

The full glory of dawn saw the division of the spoils, the loading of the heaped treasures of the decimated Zodak Horde upon the great chariots of their conquerors. So vast was the treasure-hoard the warlike Zodaki had amassed over the ages that a hundred baggage-wains of the whelmed horde were pressed into service to help bear it off to the city of Althaar. As well, the remnants of the Zodaki were loaded aboard, for Jomdath swore that in this place of blood and death the name and nation of the Zodaki should be rendered extinct. The children and women and survivors of the conquered horde would be adopted among the Jegga clans.

In all their search of the dead city, they found no trace of Thongor of Valkarth. Neither his corpse nor his accouterments could be found amidst the dead city.

And although Jomdath and his captains searched and asked and questioned their prisoners, they could find no answer to the riddle of Thongor's disappearance . . . no clue to the mystery of his whereabouts.

The only hint they could uncover was cryptic and

baffling, an enigma seemingly without solution.

It came from the sneering lips of an old Zodaki shaman, or witch-doctor, who had served in the depraved devil-worshipping and sacrificial cult of the Demon-God Xuthsarkya, the Lord of Worms. This cult of cruel torture and nightmare terror was the nearest thing to a religion the debased and bestial Zodak Horde had known.

Cackling with blood-chilling, mocking laughter, the old witch-doctor had said: "Ye search for the outlander, Thongor? Ye will not find him here!"

"Where then, old man?" Jomdath demanded sternly.

Again a mocking burst of jeering laughter fell from the withered lips of the shaman.

"Ye will find him *in the jaws of the Worm!*"

Further than this, the old witch-doctor refused to say, and no amount of urging or punishment could pry apart his silent lips, nor drive the venomous mockery from his leering eyes.

Jomdath felt a cold hand close about his heart.

By "the worm," did the malignant old witch-doctor mean the god they had worshipped? Did he mean that Thongor had been sacrificed in some unholy ritual of heathen savagery? Or did he mean the term as a synonym for Death? For in the solitary darkness of the grave, the worm alone is king.

And his brow furrowed with troublous memories. This city of immemorial Yb was sometimes called "the City of the Worm." Was it because it was the center of the depraved cult that worshipped the Lord of Worms . . . or were the whispered and shadowy myths that Jomdath had heard—true? For rumor claimed that in unknown catacombs beneath the ancient city, a hideous and fantastic Dweller in Darkness slithered through the cavernous ways it ruled . . . a monstrous and gigantic *worm*.

Jomdath continued the search for his mighty friend and lordly comrade until midday, when he finally could no longer postpone the return trek to his city of Althaar. He could find no entrance to this mysterious and perhaps legendary underworld that was rumored to exist beneath the stones of immemorial Yb. Perhaps there were no catacombs. Perhaps Thongor had been slain. . . . Although it saddened him beyond words to give over the search, he

72

was forced to do so. For his wounded warriors must be carried back to Althaar where their many hurts could be bathed and salved and bandaged.

As the great chariot caravan of the triumphant Jegga Horde rolled through the broken gates of fallen Yb and thundered out into the midst of the endless plain, Jomdath looked back at the silent ruins. He wondered if he would ever clasp the hand of Thongor in this life again.

And the leering, mocking phrase the vile old shaman had spat at him arose again to haunt his memory, as it would for days to come . . .

"Ye will find him in the jaws of the Worm!"

CHAPTER 10

THE UNDERGROUND WORLD

War's iron music shakes the plains
As Jomdath's fury breaks the foe,
But him they seek has burst his chains
To dare the unknown world below.

Where madness reigns and nature sleeps
In nightmare caves beneath the earth,
He fights the Terror of the Deeps—
Vast spawn of some unholy birth!

—*Thongor's Saga,* XVII, 15-16.

Thongor fell like a stone into a frigid gulf of whirling blackness. A damp and icy wind whistled up from the black abyss into which he hurled headfirst. The breath of the pit was foul with a slimy, musky fetor . . . a stench of indescribable decay which assaulted the senses like the sickening odor of a nest of squirming serpents, coiled amongst their own reeking wastes.

As he fell, Thongor thrust his sword into its scabbard so as to have both hands free. He had not thought the black well opened on any such enormity of depth, and thrust out his arms, hoping to seize and cling to some projection or ledge—but his hands touched nothing!

Were he to land on solid stone from such a drop, he would need the luck of the gods to survive with anything less fatal than a pair of shattered legs. . . .

Then an icy shock bathed his hurtling form, as he struck the surface of a subterranean lake and crashed below the surface to flail and flounder in lightless depths. The water was incredibly cold; at first the impact stunned him, but the biting chill of the underground waters revived him and he struck out with powerful arms, rising again to the surface choking and spluttering and numb to the bone.

He found himself in the grip of a powerful current! No lake this, but a subterranean river which swept him along head over heels with irresistible force. All about him was utter blackness so that he could see naught, but from the way the roar of the surging river rebounded and echoed, he judged that the torrent rushed through a narrow, low-roofed tunnel. To fight the seething waters would be useless, so he concentrated on merely keeping his head above water, a task sufficiently difficult to occupy his full attention for some time.

The underground river hurtled at frightful velocity through a tunnel that curved and twisted, as Thongor soon discovered when the violence of the river's force scraped him painfully against walls of rough and jagged rock at the first turn. He devised a method of kicking out with his legs whenever he sensed the current was about to swing him bruisingly against the wall again. And as he fought the river with all his strength, he grimly felt the piercing chill of the black waters deadening his mighty limbs like a creeping paralysis. Unless he managed to escape the torrent soon—very soon—the cold would numb his arms and legs beyond the power of even his iron will to force them to further exertions, and he would sink helplessly and go down to a terrible death amidst the darkness and the cold, drowned in the seething depths of this unknown river somewhere below the earth. . . .

And then, without warning of any kind, the underground torrent burst into a huge and echoing chamber as vast as the domed and vaulted nave of some stupendous cathedral. His senses caught a distant gleam of faint light—and then the current swept him with stunning impact against a rough obstruction of cold wet stone. With the last ounce of strength in his numb arms and shoulders, he seized an upper protuberance and heaved his bruised and aching body up out of the river onto a narrow ledge or flat surface of gelid stone.

He flung a length of dripping hair out of his eyes and peered around him in the thick gloom. Gradually, as he rested, his eyes adjusted to the darkness. There *was* a faint source of light, a dim, gray-greenish glow unlike any radiance he had known before. And slowly, by its feeble half-light, he began to make out the contours of his new surroundings.

About the rock he clung to, the river poured into a black lake flecked with white foam. Somewhere beyond vision to his left, this lake drained off in a waterfall of unguessable size, for the thunder of falling water filled the cavern with booming echoes and floating mist of droplets. Here and there, immense fang-like spears of slick and glassy stone knifed up from the foaming waters. Some lifted to three times the height of a standing man, and were as huge about as the girth of the giant lotifer trees of the forest country. The furious, rushing flow of the river-current had eroded and eaten away, over unthinkable centuries, the thick bases of these monstrous stalagmites, forming disk-shaped ledges of stone that overhung the gulf. It was to one of these that Thongor had hauled himself upon.

He craned his neck and peered up into the gloom above. He could not see the arched and vaulted roof that overhung the cave, but if it were low enough he might be able to grasp one of the dangling stalactites and climb up, perhaps to find his way back to the upper world again!

Off to his right, beyond a number of conical, tapering stalagmites, he saw a ledge of stone that formed the edge of the lake. It was from that direction that the faint green-gray light seemed to seep.

The nearest stalagmite was not far. Rising to his full height, clinging with one hand to the slick stone spear that had saved him from the lake's cold embrace, he managed to step across the foaming waters to the safety of the next —and thence to a further—and thus he gained the stony margin of the lake, and clambered up a steep, sharply-eroded incline, to stand on dry land again.

The ground underfoot was mostly solid stone, but heavy-littered with dust and powdered rock and chips of moldering rubble that crunched and squeaked beneath his boot-heels as he slid down the further side of the incline to the cavern proper. Here, he inched his way through a dense forest of stony stalagmites set close together. The weird glow strengthened as he worked his way towards it.

He found himself in a fantastic forest of monstrous growths. Toadstools . . . vast, bloated domes of stinking fungi that nodded at chest-height atop long warty stems as thick about as his mighty arm. About the obscene and moldy growths hovered a dim nimbus of unhealthy phosphorescence—the eerie, sourceless light he had glimpsed when first he had drawn himself up out of the chill bosom of the underground lake.

The green-gray radiance was a chemical illumination, the witch-fires of decay.

Here, some distance from the roaring waters, with a wall of stony spears rising between him and the foaming lake, he could gain some notion of the height of the cavern's groined roof. Whatever stalactites might hang downward, it seemed obvious from the height of the booming echoes that gobbled and cackled far above that the domed roof was enormously high.

He would have to seek another exit.

With the grim patience of a true barbarian, the Valkarthan began to search along the sloping walls of the vast cave.

After a weary interval of indeterminate length, he found a side-tunnel that branched off from the domed central hall. The dim phospherescence of decaying fungi did not penetrate the portal's gloom. Peer as he might, his keen gold eyes could not see beyond the curtain of darkness that stretched across the black mouth of the cavern. So, drawing his sword, he plunged into blind darkness, senses alert. The slightest sound could trigger him to a slashing attack.

But seemingly naught lived within these unlit deeps, save for the monstrous and unnaturally huge fungi of the lake-cave. He traversed the full length of the side-tunnel without encountering a living creature, and stepped forth

76

into an even vaster cathedral-dome—a gigantic echoing space that must have been a thousand yards across. So incredibly huge was it that he could not see the further wall!

But see he could, and it was with relief that his eyes blinked and drank in the fierce light of volcanic fires. Good to see by honest firelight again, after the greenish murk of sodden fungoid things!

The uneven floor of this most gigantical of caverns was filled with crater-like pits, and from many of these jets of red-gold flame roared up to towering heights. Perhaps they were geysers of natural gas, or the escape vents for some unknown region of volcanic fury far below in the earth-quake-torn bowels of the planet: at any rate, whatever their origin or nature, they provided a fiery light by which Thongor could see his surroundings clearly.

And a source of warmth, as well. He approached the nearest fire-fountain and warmed his half frozen limbs in its furnace-breath for a time, wringing dry his cloak and long unshorn mane of coarse black hair. In the baking heat of the flaming geyser, he felt the exhaustion and numb cold seep from his body and soon felt more like himself, ready to face and overcome whatever obstacle might yet arise in his path to stand between him and his escape to the upper world.

He was, however, aware of an aching void of hunger. It seemed endless hours since the last meal, and that had been only a hasty field-lunch amid the Hills of the Thunder-Crystals. He yearned for a luscious steak and wished he might come upon some succulent species of cavern-life so that he could slay it and cook its meat in the fire-jets. But, alas, this cavern also appeared sterile and devoid of living things. He could not see even the fungoid growths of the lake-cave.

When he was warm and completely dry, he began to think about moving on. He crossed the cavern of the fire-fountains and entered another tunnel which branched off in a new direction.

He soon lost all sense of time. After he had stumbled forward through cavern and open space and cavern again for some indeterminate time, he felt himself becoming so weary that he slept, ignoring the pangs of hunger, curling up on the dry warm floor of a huge long cave, rolled in his cloak, the great sword lying near his hand in case of need.

When he awoke, stiff but rested, he had no notion of how long his slumber had lasted. An hour, or a day—who could say? But the hunger that coiled within him now was a cold knot of devouring pain.

He passed through another chain of caverns, and came to a stone bridge that curved in a natural arch over a rushing river of cold black water. Whether this was the same river into which he had fallen when first entering this underground world, or a branch of it, or an entirely different stream, he had no way of telling. *But this river bore life.*

When he had come to the mid-point of the stone bridge, a snaky neck rose dripping from the black water—a neck as thick about as his waist, and scaly with plates of gray horn. The fearful head that dipped and swerved towards him, opening slavering jaws set with fangs like ivory knives, had blind white eyes.

There on the slippery arch of rock, he fought the blind river-dragon amidst the dark cave. His singing blade batted the head to one side, slashing cheek and jowl and cataract-white eye with a wound that oozed green reptilian gore.

The gray *poa* of the black river hissed like a steam-vent and struck at him, half-mad with pain, fanged jaws clashing in mid-air as Thongor ducked. He sprang to one side, almost losing his footing on the slick, wet stone, and swung the hissing blade with all the force of his mighty arms and back and shoulders behind the blow.

Fanged jaws still clashing madly, the severed head feel into the river to one side of the arch of rock, while the weaving neck, its stump spouting gore, slid into the rushing torrent on the other side.

Thongor caught up with the still-flopping corpse of the river-dragon a bit further downstream, where it had wedged between two stalagmites. It was tough work, cutting through the heavy scaly hide of the giant lizard, but hunger goaded him on, and ere long, Thongor had carved several huge slabs of meat, which he washed in the rushing water until they were drained of blood.

The next cavern was another volcanic place, this time with bubbling pools of lava instead of spouting geysers of jetting flame. After a little experimenting, he found the steaks could be satisfactorily cooked by being laid on the very edge of the bubbling ponds of sluggish, cherry-red molten rock.

He devoured his first hearty meal in untold hours with an appetite that would have flattered the chef in his palace back in Patanga. He found the dragon-steak delicious. The meat was firm and juicy, and only slightly flavored of musk. It was the first time he had ever chanced to eat dragon, and he was happy to discover it did not taste at all as foul and slimy as one might imagine.

After the meal, he curled up in the warmth of the lava-pool and slept as soundly as only a tired man with a full belly can sleep. And woke, hours later, to go forward again through the maze of catacombs and tunnels. . . .

Something was following him. It had been following him for an hour or so; at least, his first suspicions of pursuit had come an hour past.

A distant rustling, slithering sound, slow and continuous, as of some creature dragging an enormous weight over rough stone. He did not pause to wait for his unknown pursuer to catch up to him, nor did he linger so as to catch a glimpse of the rustling, slithering thing that followed him through the gulfs. He continued on at the greatest speed he could attain, hoping that which followed him would leave the trail.

He came out on an upper gallery of a gigantic domed cavern whose walls and arched roof were stained with a weird blue light that seemed to come from winking, glittering veins of some unknown mineral studding the dark rock.

The ledge whereon he stood was some score of yards above the cavern floor, and the wall was sheer and smooth. But the rustling, crawling sounds were louder and louder behind him, and the grim Valkarthan reckoned that whatever was on his trail was gaining on him fast. There was no time to loiter here on this flimsy ledge. However dangerous and difficult the descent looked, he must chance it, and soon—or find himself trapped on the protruding lip of rock, facing an unknown and bestial attacker, with a sheer fall of empty air at his back.

With Thongor, to think was to act. He dropped prone on the ledge, seizing knobs of rock, and swung himself over, seeking with booted toes a foothold on the smooth cavern wall. He found a block of weathered stone which would support his weight—but not for long—and swung down to it, leather boots sliding treacherously on the smooth, worn rock. He doubled himself up, wrapping his arms about the block, and again swung his feet loose, wedged them sideways in a slit of rock. Then he reached out, hands fumbling over the smooth rockface, searching for a handhold. The slithering, scraping sound was very loud now, and with it came a slimy stench of unbearable foulness . . . the nauseous fetor of decayed slime he had first smelled when falling into this hell-world of nightmare caverns, untold hours or days before!

He looked up as bits of crumbling rock sprinkled down on his back and shoulders, to see what had dislodged the debris from the ledge above . . . and the very blood froze in his veins with primal awe and superstitious dread!

Slithering out and over the ledge a dozen feet above him as he clung to the wall of rock was a head of gelatinous, lucent and flabby matter that reeked of slime—the head of a gigantic, blind, loathsome and terrible Worm whose length was incalculable, but whose maw, which gaped to pluck him like a fly from the wall, was a dozen feet across!

Clinging helplessly against the face of the wall, Thongor could not reach or draw his sword.

A fluid length of jelly-like substance flowed from the tunnel's mouth, as more of the Worm's stupendous length inched out upon the ledge. The blind, gaping-mouthed head swung down toward him.

CHAPTER 11

IN THE JAWS OF THE WORM-GOD

> Wide, gaping jaws before him loom—
> Cold steel hacks through its hellish face!
> Yet naught deters the Crawling Doom,
> Nor slows its steady, creeping pace. . . .
>
> He battles on as in a trance,
> Yet it ignores the bite of steel.
> How halt its slithering advance,
> How kill a Thing that cannot feel?

—*Thongor's Saga,* XVII, 17-18.

All day, Shangoth moved south across the endless plains in quest of the Zodaki warriors who had seized the Lord Thongor and carried him away from the midst of his comrades. The faithful Rmoahal ran at a steady, loping pace that devoured the miles—a pace no man less powerful than the superbly muscled young Titan could have endured for a fraction of that time without collapsing in exhaustion. Yet the enormous, steely thews of the eight-foot-tall blue-skinned giant propelled him on and on as tirelessly as a mighty engine.

He knew the Zodaki would bear their captive into the walls of immemorial Yb, the City of the Worm, and he ran unerringly toward the ruined city, guided by that strange seventh sense of direction known only to the warriors of his great race. This uncanny mental compass was Nature's protection for her Rmoahal children: without an infallible sense of direction, they would easily become lost and wander until death found them, helpless amidst the countless leagues of flat and grassy steppes. Thus, although guided by no visible signs, nor even conscious of the inward promptings that guided his path, the stalwart Prince of the

Jegga Horde flew like an arrow across the leagues of yellow grass towards distant Yb.

He paused several times to rest his mighty thews and refresh himself with a few bites from his supplies and a long drink from the waterskin that dangled from his girdle—standard war equipment of his people, who were pitted in continuous and never-ending conflict with their many foes from the hour of birth, and thus never left the shelter of their camp without each his store of food and drink.

By near evening, he came to a full stop.

Ahead of him and to the left, a monstrous zamph prowled restlessly through the long golden grasses. It was a young bull weighing about four tons, and from the looks of him he was in need of water, for he wandered stumblingly, swinging his great head from side to side as if tormented with thirst, or with some stinging pain he could not assuage. Strapped to its mighty back, the zamph bore a huge saddle ornate with gems and emblazonings. From the markings, scarcely visible through the failing light, Shangoth recognized this as one of the saddle beasts the Jegga escort had ridden when they went forth with the Lord Thongor to seek the Hills of the Thunder-Crystals. The beasts had fled when they were attacked by the invisible warriors of the Zodak Horde. This one had wandered far, and Shangoth was delighted to encounter him, for the zamph could greatly speed and shorten his journey to distant Yb.

The young warrior ran forward lightly, sounding the shrill call with which the Jegga summon their beasts. The zamph seemed to recognize the signal he had been trained to obey; however, he did not trot forward to receive a rider as he should. Instead, head lolling sluggishly, the great zamph planted all four stumpy legs wide and stood waiting, brow lowered so that the keen horn that thrust like a sword of bone from between his eyes, pointed directly at Shangoth.

The prince did not have time to question this peculiar response, for as he ran up to the beast it swerved and charged directly at him with its earth-shaking tread drumming on the plain like a mighty drumbeat. And then it was he saw the black arrow that protruded from one gory eye-socket of the beast's pain-tormented head, and knew a chance shaft had struck the helpless animal and had driven it mad with agony.

And then Shangoth knew no more—a tremendous engine of pure destruction struck him with a terrific blow that lifted him from the earth and flung his blood-splashed senseless body a dozen yards away, to thud against the earth like a trampled, broken toy.

Thongor clung helplessly to the sheer rock wall as the blind, questing head of the Devilworm came swinging down to his level. Its sphincter-like maw gaped to rip him from the wall. The fetid breath of the incredible monster blew like a stinking wind about him, rank with centuries of decaying slime. The black jaws gaped for his body, dripping with a loathsome saliva.

He knew it for a *xuth*—one of the enormous and dreaded giant worms that inhabit the moldering catacombs below the Lemurian cities. He had seen and battled against its kind six years before, in the caverns below Thurdis, when he and Ald Turmis had made a desperate escape from the hands of Thalaba the Destroyer. But this thing was vaster than belief . . . huge and swollen with unnatural growth beyond all comprehension! The xuth are enormous blind and slug-like worms of slithering foulness that haunt the deepest and blackest depths. They seize their prey in the gulping maw which sucks the victim down into a tube lined with gland-sacs which secrete a corrosive, organic acid-like digestive fluid. The dissolved flesh of the prey then penetrates the cell-walls by osmosis. The xuth are very primitive life-forms. Devoid of brain or sense-organs beyond a rudimentary sense of smell, and lacking heart or vulnerable organs or even a highly developed nervous system, they are virtually unkillable, since their slimy, gelatinous amoeboid bodies possess no sensitivity to pain and no vital spots.

These thoughts flashed through his mind in an instant, as he clung helplessly to the wall. He felt a moment of black and terrible despair that he could not draw sword to defend himself—to let go of the wall with even one hand would have dislodged him from his hold. But perhaps it was better to fall to a swift, clean death on the rocky floor below, than end in the loathsome belly of the giant worm-thing of the pits. . . .

It struck like a bolt of lightning.

The sphincter-jaws closed about his legs, and he sank into the rubbery, working mouth of the hideous Hellworm!

The light of day vanished. Jelly-like substance enveloped his body. His bare flesh stung painfully as the drooling saliva bubbled over his limbs and chest, burning like hot venom. He could feel the rippling peristaltic action as the xuth began to swallow him down the noisome, slimy channel of its throat.

It was the grimmest and most terrible moment of his entire life . . . and doubtless it would be the last.

The world swung madly about, and blood thundered in Thongor's congested temples as the stupendous Worm slithered down the side of the vertical cliff! His senses were reeling from lack of air. He opened his eyes, ignoring the stinging slime, and saw a feeble reddish gleam of the fire-fountains that pitted the cavern-floor. Their blaze penetrated the glassy, translucent flesh of the monster worm. Thongor knew he must breathe—or die.

Almost without thinking—as if the terror of the moment triggered deep within him some primal automatic survival mechanism—he tore one hand free from the sucking blubber and ripped his great sword from its scabbard with a surge of iron thews. The space within the worm-thing's gullet was too constricted to swing the blow—he lunged weakly forward and let the keen point of the cold steel slice and tear through the jellied, slimy plasmoid throat!

Fresh air and stronger light!

The sword-point had slashed through the thin wall of flesh in the throat. Thongor kicked and struggled mightily, sucking in the clean air, slashing the wound and stretching the orifice wider. Now the slithering thing had gained the cavern-floor. With a mighty burst of exertion, Thongor ripped and tore his way out of the monster, and staggered, shaken to the depths of his soul, but—free!

He sagged limply against the base of the cliff and vomited. He was befouled with slime from head to toe, and he stank abominably. But he yet lived, and had done what no mortal man had done from the beginning of time until this hour—cut his way out of the swallowing throat of a devouring monster!

The unthinkably huge worm-thing loomed near, wriggling past with a slow contracting and expanding rhythm. The tremendous wound his sword had made gaped hideously in its throat, leaking a vile and oily greenish ooze, yet the beast felt no pain—did not even seem to notice the four-foot-long wound carved in its flesh!

But in some occult manner, the foul thing sensed his nearness. The blind, eyeless head swung slowly towards him and the drooling sphincter worked slobberingly.

He ran some way out into the center of the vast cavern, hoping to outdistance the slow-moving and mindless thing. But when he looked back, the huge, slithering monster of the depths was crawling after him in ponderous and inexorable pursuit.

Weak, sick, shaken, Thongor yet turned to fight the worm-thing. He swung a terrific back-handed blow with the full strength of his mighty shoulders—a blow that would have disemboweled a full-grown zamph! It laid open a great slash of the worm's jelly-like flesh. A flap of half-severed worm-meat hung wobbling, like a huge slab of translucent stinking gelatin. And although the ghastly wound ran with watery green slime blood, the monster yet advanced upon him tirelessly, as remorseless as doom itself. Thongor fought on, slashing it about the face.

One wound laid open the ring of muscle that worked the maw's contracting sphincter. The rubbery valve-muscle was cut through and the mouth hung open, powerless to close—but even that wound caused the xuth no pain!

He dodged around a stalagmite thick as a tree-trunk and gained the very center of the cavern, momentarily outdistancing the huge but sluggish creature. And there before him rose a grim object. A huge cube of dull black stone, marked with uncouth glyphs in some lost, forgotten tongue. He blinked at it curiously, noticing how its surface was befouled with reeking slime and stained with enormous grisly splotches of black, caked, dry blood. Something crunched underfoot and he glanced down. The floor about the black cube was littered with bones and human skulls—dry and yellow, and curiously smooth, as if eaten by some powerful acid. . . .

Slowly, comprehension dawned within him, and his weary face hardened grimly. Here it was the depraved and soulless Zodaki worshipped their Devil-God, *the Titanic Worm!* Revulsion gripped him. He could picture all too clearly the thousands of naked, screaming victims chained helpless on that grisly altar while chanting beasts in human form summoned to its nameless feast the loathly worm!

He turned. The xuth was still coming after him, and between him and it was only an intermittent geyser of flaming gas, now quiescent.

His lips spread in a fighting grin, for now he knew the way. Instead of fleeing further, he walked *toward* the oncoming worm. Cold steel had failed to halt the Worm-God's slow advance—his keen wits might yet prove sharper than his sword's glittering edge! He took a stand on the lip of the smoking well. The blind, drooling visage of the xuth stared at him only a dozen yards away. He tried to recall how long it had been since last he had noticed the geyser spurt—*ah!*

Even as he had dared to hope, the Worm-God lifted its squirming body into the air and arched above the silent, smoking pit to swoop down on him. He sprang backwards hastily, and fell stumbling to his knees as the immense shadow of the Worm's head fell across him. Then a wave of searing heat baked his bare arms as he sprawled. A hideous crackling, frying sound thundered in his ears. He rolled over on his back and looked upon a sight to freeze the marrow of a man's soul.

The Hellworm had arched its titanic length across the small blackened pit, the head questing slowly from side to side, hanging above the ground. And the geyser *flamed!* A tremendous jet of white-hot flame squirted up, catching the worm's arched length in the full force of its fiery fountain!

As he watched, the flesh sizzled, roasting in the blast, burning like a stupendous living torch. The slimy, watery, amoeboid flesh of the age-old Worm-God shriveled—blackened, flaking away in seconds—and burned, as some flammable element in its vile flesh ignited.

Wrapped in a sheath of flame, the hundred-foot worm writhed and struggled madly on the stone floor of the vast cavern. Now it felt pain in very truth. Even while the searing flame ate inward, it slithered and writhed in an insane fury of mindless and unendurable agony!

Thongor watched with somber eyes as the monstrous xuth died.

Beyond the cavern of the altar, he found yet another of the underground streams and bathed his sore, aching body in the icy waters, gladly cleansing the foul slime from his flesh. Then he went on, intending to forge ahead so long as strength endured within his body.

He did not get far.

As he passed a side-tunnel, a flashing movement in the gloom of the tunnel's mouth caught his eye. A globe of thin glass flashed in the light to splinter to fragments at his feet.

A vaporous cloud of perfumed blue powder swirled up to envelope him before he could move.

Without thinking, he drew a breath—drew the narcotic dust into his lungs. And strength ebbed from his limbs. He fell forward into a spreading pool of whirling blackness and lay like a dead thing.

A portion of the shadow detached itself from the mouth of the tunnel and resolved into a tall man in robes of midnight black, hooded and visored from view.

It was the Black Archdruid, Mardanax of Zaar!

He had journeyed hither in winged flight to take his captive from the Zodak Horde. With unearthly magic arts he had tracked the Valkarthan through the weird maze of catacombs . . . to render him senseless with the narcotic vapors of the Dream Lotus.

And now Thongor, mightiest of warriors, kingliest of heroes, lay totally helpless at the feet of his greatest and most relentless enemy.

Eyes of cold and mocking cruelty smiled through black mask-slits, as Mardanax of Zaar leaned over Thongor's unconscious body, and prodded him in the side with one foot.

Then, chuckling gloatingly, he stooped over the fallen hero and kicked him deliberately in the face.

CHAPTER 12

WINGED DRAGONS OF ZAAR

He lures through flame that Worm of Hell,
Wherein it perishes . . . but he,
Ensorcelled by the Druid's spell
Is flown to Zaar beside the sea.

—*Thongor's Saga,* XVII, 19.

Cold wind rushing past his face roused Thongor. He shook his head groggily, his shaggy mane of coarse black hair whipping out behind him on the wind, streaming like a heavy silk banner. The spell of the narcotic powder slowly loosened its hold on his brain, and his wits cleared. He gazed down to find himself hurtling through the sky, thousands of yards above the surface of the earth!

For a moment, his mind still clouded with the blue dust of the Dream Lotus, the barbarian thought he had been slain there in the lightless crypts and caverns beneath the City of the Worm—thought for one flashing, terrible instant that his soul was now borne heavenward on the winged steeds of the War Maids who carried the spirits of fallen heroes into the Shadowlands, to the halls of Father Gorm.

But then he saw that he was strapped into a great saddle astride a fantastic monster whose mighty bat-like wings rose and fell, bearing him through the sky like a god! He had seen and fought such winged dragons before. He recognized the long snaky neck, the hawk-like head with its cruel hooked beak and crest of bristling spines. He looked up at the moving shadow of the leathery, clawed wings that must have spanned a full forty feet from tip to tip, and felt his thighs press against the scaled torso of the flying monster. Behind, the monster's body trailed away into a long barbed tail that lashed against the wind.

It was a dreaded lizard-hawk, the terrible dragon of the

Lemurian skies, the fearful pterodactyl of the prehistoric age whose monstrous shape and ferocious hunger made its memory linger long in the dark legends of mankind as the prototype of the mighty flying dragon of myth.

But this winged dragon wore a saddle and bridle!

A terrific shriek sounded from behind. Thongor turned in his bonds to see hovering behind him yet a second lizard-hawk, its great bat wings shadowing the sky. And the second dragon, too, wore a saddle—and had a rider. The rushing wind of their flight made his vision blur, but the Valkarthan could faintly make out a robed and masked figure in midnight black who rode the devil-dragon of the clouds like some magic steed . . . and then Thongor remembered the shadowy figure he had glimpsed in the black mouth of the cavern, just before the gush of narcotic powder had sucked him down into a whirling vortex of blackness.

And he knew that he was in the hands of the Black City of Zaar. No force but the power of black magic could tame and break to the bridle the fierce flying monsters on which he and his cloaked captor now rode.

He turned back facing forward again, examining his bonds. With great cunning, the masked magician had tied his hands and arms with strips of rawhide. The tough leather flexed slightly as great thews swelled across his broad shoulders and deep chest—stretched, but did not break. His lips tightened grimly: ropes or even chains his iron strength might have burst, but wet rawhide shrinks as it dries, and the bonds he wore cut into his flesh, numbing even his mighty muscles.

He was helpless—for now.

He looked about him through the cloud-torn sky. The sun of afternoon lingered on the horizon, filling the notches of the mountains with liquid gold and casting level shafts of ruby brilliance that stretched long purple shadows across the endless plains. From the position of the sun he knew the direction in which they flew—to the south.

And far to the south lay the grim walls and dark bastions of Zaar, the City of Magicians!

Now he knew he had been right in guessing from what source the warriors of the Zodak Horde had procured the cloaks of invisibility they had used to capture Thongor.

The warning of the Nineteen Gods Who Rule The World had been true. The Magicians of Zaar were his secret foes. By some unearthly magic they had known of his coming into these eastern lands, and plotted with their allies the Zodaki to seize the Lord of Patanga!

But—for what evil purpose did the masked magician fly him south to the Black City? For torture—a vile death —revenge for the destruction of Adamancus and Thalaba the Destroyer—retribution for his victory over the Druid Brotherhoods of Patanga and Tsargol? His gold eyes narrowed; his lips thinned as muscles grew taut along his lean jaw. Thongor of Valkarth did not fear death as did most city-bred men, raised amidst the soft luxuries of what they called "civilization." Nay—Thongor was sprung of a rugged stock, and throughout his savage youth he had lived daily with the grim specter of death as a constant companion. Death was an old comrade, and the Shadowlands bore no terrors that could daunt his stout heart.

But what of his realm of Patanga, with him slain? What of his beloved princess and his young son? He knew the gods held his life of great importance, groomed him for some mighty role in the events of the future. *With Thongor slain, might not the Black Magicians of Zaar overwhelm the bright young cities of the West?* His grim, impassive features tightened and his strange gold eyes blazed with cold fires. Helpless he might be now, but he must watch and wait to seize the opportunity to escape whenever that chance should present itself. . . .

Now the lands over which they flew slowly became harsh and barren. Thick meadow grasses fell away, exposing scab-like patches of dead dry soil. Even the fresh wind grew sour, tainted with metallic fumes. The nearer they came to the Black City, the more stark and dead and barren nature became. It was as if they approached some vile center of contagion, some dark focus of cosmic forces of destruction and decay.

Ere the conflagration of sunset had consumed the last red embers of day, they hurtled above a dead plain of sterile rock and poisoned earth, as lifeless and grim as must be the frozen deserts of the moon.

And then Thongor saw the Black City of Zaar itself. It stood at the end of a long rocky promontory that thrust out into the Unknown Sea. Cold waves advanced, collapsed in thunder, and retreated again, withdrawing into the bosom of the great ocean. But again and ever again the mighty waves swept forward to dash in a fury of exploding spray against beaches of black crystal sand and to roar in frustrate foam about the stupendous wall that held back the remorseless waters of the deep.

For this remotest southeastern edge of Lemuria was already crumbling beneath the unconquerable will of Nature. Already, in this most ancient part of the Lost Continent, the destined and irreversible submergence of the continent had begun. Were it not for the mighty sea wall of black marble the magicians had erected against the sea, the Black City would be deep fathoms below the cold waves of the storm-torn and everlasting main.

They circled above the most ancient inhabited city of man, and Thongor gazed upon it with grim, searching eyes.

Zaar was built like a mighty fortress upon its promontory. Great walls of black glassy substance ringed it in; the squat towers and ziggurats of strong citadels rose amid its narrow winding streets. And as he gazed upon Zaar, the heart failed within him. For no army ever raised by man could penetrate those beetling walls or win entrance past those frowning bastions. . . .

A dead river of salty, acid water ran through the black metropolis in caverns far below the cobbled streets. It emerged from a barred grill in the city wall, foul with nameless refuse and beslimed with excrement. A dun pall of seething smoke hovered above the dark palaces—the noisome breath of wizard furnaces and strange laboratories. It was like some ebon city built upon the sooty plains of hell . . . and into this terrible realm of evil and sorcery, he must venture—alone, friendless, and bound.

Even Thongor's stalwart courage quailed at the thought.

Then, at some unseen, unheard signal from the masked magician who rode behind him, Thongor's dragon-steed arched mighty wings against the stars and swept down over the walled city in a lowering spiral. The Black City swung up towards them, lurid with torch-lit streets, winding ways and vast avenues that twisted between mountainous piles of cyclopean architecture. He could see red flames glaring with ghastly luminance from peaked gothic windows and barred gates like grinning dragon-jaws.

Ponderous ziggurats and spires of crimson and jet swung past as the winged dragon arrowed down towards the flame-lit heart of the dark metropolis of necromancy, bearing the helpless Thongor bound into the very stronghold of his enemies.

At the heart of the Black City a tremendous ziggurat loomed tier upon tier into the night sky like a man-made mountain of colossal thickness. Toward this central pile Thongor's mount sped on flapping wings. From the square topmost tower of the squat structure a black opening belched scarlet fire that filled the night with intermittent flares of fiery light and rolling clouds of sooty smoke.

Upon one of the broad tiered levels of the central ziggurat the two winged dragons descended, coming to rest on massive spars of dull red crystal that thrust out over the torch-lit streets below like angular gargoyles. The pterodactyls settled on these huge spars for all the world like hunting falcons coming to roost on stands.

The tier was broad and level as a mighty avenue. Robed, silent figures gravely observed their descent from stations along wall and tower-crest. As Thongor sat upright, bound in the saddle, two of the hooded men approached at the silent command of the masked magician and unfastened the Valkarthan's bonds, permitting him to dismount from the precarious dragon-roost overhanging the street.

As they assisted him to the security of the broad tier, Thongor scrutinized the hooded ones narrowly. It had been difficult to ascertain their race with face and body enveloped in the shroud-like robes, but upon closer examination Thongor perceived them to be of the same brown-skinned, black-eyed and lean-limbed Turanian race as were his people of Patanga.

Now the masked magician dismounted and Thongor was able to discover the means by which the sorcerers of Zaar had gained mastery over the untamed monsters of this primitive age. One gloved hand reached within the magician's hood and withdrew, having unclasped from about his brows a thin wire headband of ruddy orichalc to which were affixed strange seals and talismans of an unknown green-glowing metal. The moment the sigils were removed from the brows of Mardanax, the dragons became restive.

The one nearest to the Black Archdruid clashed its beak, arched its snaky neck, and hissed like a steam-whistle.

One of the black-robed guards received the headband from the masked magician and clasped it about his own brows. The larger sigil rested squarely in the middle of the forehead, in the position of that organ of occult power known to the annals of sorcery as the *Ajnaic Chakra*—the "third eye." Other, lesser talismans were bound tight to the hollows of the temples, and at the rear of the head near the base of the skull, close to the mysterious pineal gland, while the fifth sigil was affixed to the crown of the head, the site of that astral counterpart of the cortical layer of the brain, the *Sahasraraic Chakra*—"the thousand-petaled Lotus."

The moment the hooded guard mounted this weird wire cap on his brows and turned his attention to the hissing, angry lizard-hawk, the creature quieted, became dormant, put its head under one bat wing and—slept!

Thongor's strange gold eyes narrowed thoughtfully. It would seem that the five sigils somehow intensified and focused the thought-waves of the human brain, empowering a mind thus magnified to seize and control the more rudimentary brain of a beast. His flesh crept at the thought. With such a device at their control, the unscrupulous Black Magicians of Zaar could place a fantastic flying army of pterodactyls under their command, turning them against their foes—could launch a herd of jungle dragons, the titanic saurians of the swamp country, against the walls of any city which remained antagonistic to their demands. With such a secret they could conquer the world!

He stood spread-legged on the broad tier of the ziggurat, turning cold watchful eyes on his two robed and hooded guards. This might be the moment to turn and strike, to attempt an escape—surely, he was now guarded by fewer enemies than he would be when immured within this mountain-like citadel!

But each guard bore a long wand or staff tipped with black metal carved in the likeness of a demon's claw, clutching a rough sphere of smoky crystal filled with flickering, coiling witch-fires of evil green radiance.

Thongor gazed at these innocuous-seeming staves, and knew them for what they were—and knew, as well, that

93

escape would be hopeless. For those clouded gems were sithurls. And from their settings, he knew them for the paralyzing-weapons which could benumb a man's thews at a single touch, steal the strength from his limbs with a glancing blow. Set in just such a fashion had been the paralysis-sithurl he had first seen years before, when the cruel hand of the shaman Tengri wielded it to render helpless the great war chief of the Jegga Nomads, the mighty Jomdath.

His head sank slowly on his broad chest. Hopeless . . . helpless!

The masked magician turned to the guards.

"Conduct our prisoner, the Lord Thongor, hence from this place unto the Hall of the Nine Thrones, where he shall stand before the Lords of Zaar for judgment!"

"Aye, Elder One."

Thongor turned and strode with them across the windswept tier of stone, lit by the tossing plume of scarlet flames far above, and entered into the central ziggurat without protest.

And thus did Mardanax the Black Archdruid bear Thongor the Lord of the West prisoner into the City of Magicians, to face a doom stranger than any mortal man had ever faced before. . . .

CHAPTER 13

SHANGOTH THE AVENGER

And all the while, to find his friend,
The Jegga prince hath crossed the plain
To where the very land doth end
And somber Zaar confronts the main.

—*Thongor's Saga*, XVII, 20.

When he came to his senses at last, after uncounted hours of unconsciousness, the prince of the Jegga Nomads found himself lying stiff and bruised and covered with dried

94

blood. The enraged zamph that had attacked him was nowhere to be seen—doubtless the pain-maddened beast had wandered off somewhere out of sight.

Shangoth clambered laboriously to his feet and stood swaying, staring blearily about him. His head throbbed like a beaten gong, spreading waves of bright scarlet pain through his aching brain. He lifted one unsteady hand to his brows and felt wetness and raw flesh. The blow of the zamph's horn had laid open his scalp in an ugly wound. Had it not been for the tremendous stamina of Shangoth's powerful young body, and the superb health enjoyed by this splendid young specimen of fighting manhood, he might well have never recovered consciousness. As it was, although the Rmoahal's magnificent physique had managed to throw off most of the effects of the wounds inflicted by the monstrous zamph when it had charged, thrown and trampled him hours or days before, the demands had drawn deeply on his reserves of vital energy and he felt weak as a sick girl. He swayed, staggered, hand to brow, fighting for consciousness against the waves of throbbing darkness that threatened to engulf him again.

Despite the urgency of his mission, he quite realistically assessed his chances of catching up with Thongor's captors in his present weakened condition as virtually nonexistent. He therefore resolved to rest himself, treat his wounds and regain his strength, before pressing forward—and with the practicality and singleness of purpose of the savage he wasted no time in doing just that.

A bundle of dry grasses set alight with flint and steel from the pocket-pouch of his harness gave him warmth and light against the night chills. Water from his belt-canteen, heated in his helm, enabled him to wash his body clean of blood, and to cleanse the gaping wound in his brow, which he then treated with the remarkable healing salve his people had used for untold ages, a medicinal preparation whose curative powers were but little short of the miraculous. Then, as he rested, absorbing warmth from the crackling fire, he delved into his store of field rations, concocting a nourishing meal of jellied fruits and spiced dry meats, washed down with a heady draught or two of native wine.

Then, wrapped in his warm cloak, he slept beside the fire

through the long chill night rousing with the fresh salt tang of the morning wind keen in his nostrils, feeling marvelously invigorated, his powers restored to near their normal strength.

As the first rays of dawn stroked the high-piled clouds to fiery gold, he set forth on Thongor's trail. Perforce he must follow it on foot, since he had sighted no steed save for the maddened zamph with the arrow in its eye that had savaged him hours or days before. But the robust strength of his magnificent young body propelled him tirelessly forward at a steady and unvarying pace through the long hours of morning.

When the sun had nearly ascended to the noonward zenith, he came upon the broken walls of the dead city of Yb, his goal.

And found, instead of the camp of his enemies—a conquered stronghold, a decimated fortress, strewn with the bloody leavings of a battlefield!

His sharp eyes soon spotted the Jegga tribal markings on fallen arrows and broken shields, and the keen-witted young warrior swiftly reconstructed the events that had left the City of the Worm a crimson shambles, reeking like a slaughterhouse.

But what of *Thongor?*

He made entry through the broken, fallen gates of the dead city and rapidly traversed the rubble-strewn streets towards the central plaza. To every side lay fallen bodies. Sword, spear and arrow, and the trampling feet of war zamph and scythe-wheeled chariot had reaped a bloody harvest here. Naught he saw that yet lived in all this immense ruin, save for a few starved mongrel curs growling over raw fragments of the fallen, and ungainly carrion birds that flapped screaming away as he came near.

In the central square he came upon the corpse of Zarthon the Terrible. His sprawled cadaver, in all the gore-splattered and barbaric magnificence of its jeweled splendor, was hideous. Unza, the flesh-eating rodents of the ruined cities, had gnawed his ugly visage into a fretted mask of bloody horror. And between his cold brows, a scarlet arrow thrust up against the noon.

Shangoth could read the markings upon the arrow, and knew it for a shaft flown from the great war-bow of his proud sire, Jomdath the mighty chief. Had, then, the Jegga rescued Thongor?

He left the corpse of the fallen chief of the Zodak Horde, and prowled further in this wilderness of ruin and death. Soon he came upon a great war zamph whose bridle and reins bore Zodaki markings. The huge beast was unharmed, its dull bluish hide free of wounds. It stood forlornly without the zamph pens, which were locked against it, patiently waiting for its master to come and give it food and drink . . . a master who must have been one of the thousands who fell before the spears of the Jegga onslaught.

As Shangoth came up to its side, the great lumbering zamph hooted plaintively and butted the horned, beaked massiveness of its great head gently against his shoulder. The young warrior of the Jegga thumped its burly shoulder and let down the barred gate to the pens. As the great brute ambled in on ponderous bowed legs, he ascertained that plentiful supplies of fresh water were in the deep trough, and ladled out the corn and bran mush that was the beast's food. It buried its beaked snout to the eyes in the water trough and drank noisily. Then it raised its dripping head and snorted in his direction, as if to say "thanks." As it fed, Shangoth regarded it thoughtfully. Finding the beast tractable and unwounded was a stroke of excellent luck . . . if his search for Thongor took him further afield than he had already come, the young bull would serve as his steed.

At that precise moment came the sign he was looking for.

A fantastic shadow darkened the sky.

He looked up to see an incredible sight—*grakk!*

Two of the feared lizard-hawks clove the bright air on thunderous hooked wings, their long snaky necks arched high, wriggling serpent-tails lashing the air-currents and massive clawed limbs folded against belly-plates as the scaly bodies soared high above the dead city of Yb.

Shangoth froze within the shadow of the pens. The terrible flying dragons of ancient Lemuria dwelt in the mountain countries of Mommur and Ardath, and were but rarely encountered here on the measureless plains of the remotest East. Yet Shangoth had heard tales of their savage ferocity and berserk fury of blood-lust—and he well knew that the flying monsters were too heavily mailed with serpent scales of tough horn to be slain by aught but the luckiest and most skillful of warriors.

It seemed that Tiandra the Goddess of Fortune still favored the prince of the Jegga, for the winged demons of the sky flapped by overhead without swooping for him with lashing barbed tail and razoring claws. They hurtled past, rising into the afternoon sky, and soon vanished from sight to the south.

But not before he glimpsed their two riders.

The heart swelled mightily within Shangoth's brawny chest. Thongor yet lived! He slumbered beneath some magic spell, slumped helplessly in the tight bonds that fastened him into the lizard-hawk's saddle, and he had not yet regained consciousness to recognize Shangoth far below—but the keen eyes of the blue-skinned Nomad Prince had recognized his friend even at such a distance. And Shangoth had seen too the black-robed form of the masked magician who rode the grakk behind the unconscious Thongor. That, and the southerly direction into which the two devil-dragons had flown, told Shangoth the destination of the two as clearly as if it had been inscribed across the breadth of the afternoon sky in gigantic letters of flame—Black Zaar!

And Shangoth must follow, even if the path led him within the grinning jaw-like gates of that evil and ill-rumored City of the Black Magicians of Chaos!

Shangoth could not know that Thongor had been seized and stunned by magic in the unknown crypts and catacombs of the cavern-world far below the City of the Worm. He could not know that the masked magician had magically transported his captive to the upper surface again, where saddled dragons waited in hiding for their master's return. These things were unimportant. He knew only that Thongor still lived, although a prisoner helpless in the chains of the cruel Black Druids—and he knew that he must pursue the flying dragons and do his utmost to rescue his mighty comrade or fall in the attempt.

When the zamph had finished his meal and drunk his fill, Shangoth too seized the opportunity to replenish his store of food supplies from the ownerless stock of provender within the homes of the slaughtered Zodak Horde. Then he swung up into the curved natural saddle of the zamph, that great saddle-shaped shield of massive bone that served to protect this Lemurian version of the prehistoric triceratops' neck and shoulders. He took up the reins and tugged the beast about. It ambled through the rubble-cluttered streets, out through the broken gates of the ruined city of Yb, and gained the windswept immensity of the great plains where its ponderous stride lengthened and carried it and its brave rider deeper and ever deeper into the South.

Shangoth reigned in the zamph on the rocky bluffs overhanging the dead river and looked down through the surly glow of sunset at the terrific panorama of immemorial Zaar.

It had taken the loyal Nomad far longer to traverse the immensity of the plains astride his lumbering zamph than it had taken Thongor and the masked magician to travel the same distance through the ways of the upper air. But, though the sky had purpled with night's overshadowing wings, Shangoth had ridden on. And when the sky crimsoned with bright dawn, still he had not paused to rest. Now, as sunset lay in flame athwart the western sky, he had reached the black walls of his goal. He stared down at the dark metropolis of sorcery. Somewhere within those grim walls lay Thongor the Mighty, a captive to the worshippers of Chaos. And only Shangoth of the Jegga stood between the Lord of the West and a terrible doom.

But how could one man, even so splendid a warrior as the eight-foot-tall Rmoahal prince, battle an entire city of evil magic?

How could he even *enter* the Black City?

He stared at the beetling grandeur of the enormous wall, bristling with watch-towers. The top of the city's wall was so broad a road had been built there, and a two-man chariot could make an entire circuit of the city atop her stupendous walls. Silent, watchful hooded men armed with strange glowing instruments stood at posts along the wall's crest, peering down at gate and road and the measureless plains beyond. And even Shangoth's bold heart sank within his breast.

He could not *climb* the wall; it towered more than a hundred feet into the sunset sky and was not built of blocks of stone where fingers and toes might find crevices wherewith to ascend, but was fashioned by fire magic all of one piece from a black vitreous substance unknown to the Nomad warrior.

He could not enter the gates, for they were gigantic barriers of solid iron red with rust, trebly locked and barred with night, so thick and strong no battering-ram or siege engine could penetrate them by sheer force alone.

How, then, could he enter?

"Where force or agility fail, one must use cunning."

Those wise words from *The Scarlet Edda* came echoing into his mind as he sat there astride the patient zamph, musing thoughtfully on the problem. As it happened, even as that phrase rang through his mind, his eyes were following the curved path of the sterile river as it cut through its deep channel across the sooty, cinder-strewn plain, to vanish beneath the walls of the Black City. . . .

He grunted with surprise, and peered more closely at the spot where the dead river ran into and beneath the vitreous walls of black glass. A low arched opening cut the surface of the wall; heavy bars of rust-red iron combed through the rushing black waters of the stream, stretching from the upper arch of the portal down to its hidden underside. And Shangoth knew exactly how he was going to enter the dread City of Magicians.

But first he removed the reins and bridle from the friendly zamph who had served him so uncomplainingly on his long journey across the immense plains. He unclipped the rings that pierced its tender ears and sensitive underlip and threw these away, so that the beast could wander free. It hooted and butted its mighty head against him inquiringly. He slapped it on one burly, rounded shoulder and pushed it away. The zamph peered questioningly at him from its mild little pig-eyes, honked again, and ambled off. He stood looking after the great beast for a time, he felt sorry to see it go. It was the last friendly creature he might see for a long time. But he could not leave the dumb brute tethered here while he sought to penetrate the Black City, for he might not live to return and release it. . . .

He dove from the bluff into the dark cold salty waters and came up gasping. The dead river was brackish, alkaline; naught could live within its icy floods. He swam toward the great city, hoping that in the dim sunset light his blue hide would not be visible against the black water. But just to be sure, he dove deep beneath the surface and swam underwater to the iron grill that barred his way. The iron rods were as thick as his thigh, but rust had eaten deeply into them during the countless centuries they had stood here in the rushing waters, and Shangoth's strength was more than twice that of a human. He dove deep and swam beneath the black waters.

He did not come up again.

CHAPTER 14

CITY OF A THOUSAND MARVELS

Accurst metropolis! Of old,
The Kings of Chaos bought thy heart,
But not with shining gifts of gold—
With foul, unholy, blackest Art!

The Demon Princes taught thee well,
Who sought to shatter Heaven's plan.
And yet the loathsome Lords of Hell
Know not the inmost soul of Man. . . .

—*Thongor's Saga*, XVII, 21-22.

Thongor followed the masked magician into the titanic ziggurat and through a maze of galleries and chambers that honeycombed the enormous structure. All about him to every side lay proof that the Black Magicians of Zaar were the masters of an incredible science-magic unguessed by the men of the outside world.

The galleries and chambers were illuminated by artificial light. Globes of cold white fire hovered motionless in midair near the ceilings of the rooms through which he passed, casting a shadowless cold luminance that drove away the darkness. These weird spheres of frozen flame were neither crystals nor hollow balls of glass. It was as if some uncanny force had gathered into one place the dim phosphorescent mists of the dank swamplands and compressed their impalpable radiance into a sphere. The Valkarthan could not guess how this strange art was accomplished; neither could he imagine how they were hung motionless in the air; nevertheless, they were there, and provided uncanny light that did not flicker nor burn low.

They passed through a high gallery that overlooked a vast hall two stories deep. There a multitude of men were busied about indescribable tasks. Thongor peered over the rail curiously. Long tables of some unknown substance white as porcelain, but transparent, covered the floor of this enormous hall. Stationed in a ring in the center were towering furnaces of heavy metal wherein searingly brilliant fires seethed at temperatures approximating those of the surface of the sun itself. Workers strangely robed in thick garments of spun silvery metal probed and manipulated long glassy rods within the core of the scintillant fires. Thongor guessed that here some weird alchemy was at work, and that the supernal heat of the sunfires were at work within the metallic crucibles, altering the very inner structure of matter itself into strange new substances. Bombarded by the intolerable radiance, the building-blocks of matter could be broken down and reformed into minerals without name, substances unknown to the world of nature.

They passed on, and came to a long low-ceilinged room where colossal tanks of green glass bubbled with strange colored fluids. Glass tubes looped and whorled in curious patterns, collecting the condensation of nameless precipitates. Here men went clad in papery suits and wore weird glass masks against the malignant vapors and corrosive fumes and deadly acids wherewith they labored, brewing potent poisons and ardent liquors for use in torment and conflict. Although he maintained an impassive visage like a face carved from hard bronze, Thongor inwardly winced with loathing that so deep an insight into the structure of the cosmos and the laws regulating nature should be perverted and twisted away from man's service to his destruction.

The laboratory workers in their strange robes and inhuman masks, toiling against green fires and amidst swirling fumes, no longer resembled human beings. They were like evil demons from the nether pits of hell, stroking the terrible furnaces of their darkling realm of torment and despair.

In other galleries, Thongor saw the secret forces of nature laid bare so that the probing mind of man might search out its hidden laws and twist it into strange forms. Captive lightning, caught in unimaginable traps and torn out of the heart of heaven, writhed like sparkling serpents of blue fire between globes of polished brass, filling the air with the metallic stench of ozone. Nameless acids and odorous chemicals were subjected to the relentless bombardment of intense forces. In a long tank of porcelain, a broth of oily fluids seethed beneath a ceaseless shower of electric sparks. Perhaps the dark intelligences of Zaar were blasphemously seeking to duplicate that accident or miracle of nature wherein life was first created.

In another laboratory of hell he saw naked slaves stretched out on operating tables while their skulls were sawn away and the pulpy brains scooped from within. These brains were then immersed in a cloudy fluid while thin wires of burning copper were inserted into key nerve centers. Noting his attention to this grisly rite, the masked magician smiled coldly.

"We seek to learn how the brain of a man may safety be removed from his body and preserved," he stated. He pointed one lean black-gloved hand to a row of platinum cannisters which were being sterilized in baths of searing steam.

"When the brain is alive and active again, we hope to preserve it within these durable containers, connecting the centers of sense and speech to certain clever mechanisms that duplicate the actions of our natural organs, so that a man's brain can be taken from his body and kept alive, still seeing, thinking and speaking. When we have perfected the art of doing this, our mightiest intellects need never fall prey to death. When at last old age overtakes the body of a man, the mind can live on, still thinking and working aeons after the body that bore it has decayed to dust. In other words, we seek absolute immortality! Think of it, savage—to preserve the mind of a man for thousands, yea, or millions of years after his body has died!"

His voice rang out, thrilling with cold fanaticism, but

Thongor's lips twisted in a grimace of disgust.

"The mind lives, the body dies," he growled. "And tell me, Druid—what of the soul?"

Cold mockery gleamed from the green eyes hidden by the black mask. "In all our anatomical researches, I fear we have not discovered the seat of that elusive component." The masked magician smiled. They went on.

It was like a tour of the armories of hell. Thongor was shown weapons that man would not rediscover in ten thousand years and more. In a huge barracks-like room he watched the cold-faced war-wizards of Zaar practicing with sithurl-tipped wands, the crystals whereof were attuned to the frequency of the human nervous system so that a slightest touch of the glowing gems grazing against bare flesh would send one's opponent shrieking and wriggling to the ground while unendurable agony blazed through his body, demolishing his brain and wrecking the very inner citadel of reason itself.

He looked upon vapor bombs, dumbbell-shaped missiles of fragile glass which bore coiled and compressed within them poisonous vapors a thousand times the strength of that blue dust of the Dream Lotus that had felled him back in the caverns of the worm—narcotic fumes of such inconceivable potency that men who breathed the slightest whiff of the vapors would die raving mad, their minds destroyed with intolerable visions and hallucinations.

They showed him warriors clad in unbreakable armor of synthetic metal as lucent as the finest glass—armor as light as thin crystal, but against which the mightiest spear or javelin would shatter—glass mail which would turn and crack the steel of a tempered sword!

He looked upon a corps of flying warriors fitted out with body harness plated with urlium, the anti-gravitic metal from which the mighty airboats of Patanga gained their flying power. His blood ran cold at the thought that the lost science of Oolim Phon had been rediscovered by these malignant and depraved sorcerors with their lust for world-conquest. Soon, soon they would turn their uncanny science to the manufacture of a great flying navy to rival even the Air Guard of Patanga!

And he saw hellish laboratories where men were injected

with narcotic poisons in gigantic dosages which rendered them totally insensible to pain.

"Imagine if you can a mighty army of such warriors," Mardanax commented in his cold mocking way. "They would fight on to the last, even as their limbs were hacked from their bodies. Of course, the dosages we use are deadly, and drive the warriors berserk, but thus they may be commanded in suicidal assaults, since they are already dying even as they fight! Shortly we shall enslave the Blue Nomads of the plains—your friends of the Jegga first of all, and then the Shung and the Thad, and the rest. Our drugs intensify their bodily strength even as they paralyze their ability to experience pain. We shall launch these slave-armies against the citadels of the West in such numbers that the West will be won without the loss of a single life of Zaar!"

Thongor made no reponse, but a low bestial growl rose unbidden from his deep chest. The Black Archdruid laughed sardonically, and guided him on through this maze of horrors.

He came at last to the very core of the manmade mountain. Here the incredible science of the Black Druids had tapped the tremendous volcanic fury that raged in the earth's center, using it as a source of motive power. The volcanic fires were stoked and fed and trapped to turn gigantic wheels, their excess flames permitted at length to escape via the gigantic shaft that ran up through the full height of the stupendous ziggurat to its topmost tier, escaping in a scarlet plume of flaming gas from that square black chimney Thongor had seen when the winged dragon had borne him down over the metropolis of evil.

Here men in heatproof armor labored above lakes and geysers of incandescent lava, amidst corrosive fumes and poisonous vapors that would have seared their unprotected bodies to husks of ash within seconds were they mad enough to go unshielded. It was like some vision of the Ultimate Pit, the squat, inhuman forms of the suited workers stalking grotesquely amidst sheets of blinding flame and titanic jets of blazing gas! Thongor viewed the incredible scene from an airtight window of heavy heat-resistant glass, but the dazzling light of the fire-lake was unnerving. As Mardanax boasted of the feat by which the Druids had harnessed the incalculable forces that seethed and raged within the volcanic depths of the planet, Thongor grimly wondered if this fantastic marvel whereby men tampered with the gigantic forces that moved and shaped the very face of the earth itself could be in part responsible for the slow submergence of the ancient Continent of Lemura. He had seen that the land of the promontory on which the dark city reared its ziggurats and pinnacles had already begun to sink beneath the mighty sea which was held back from the metropolis only by the tremendous strength of the mighty sea wall their science had erected. It would be a grim and fitting jest if by their very scientific arts the Black Magicians of Zaar had laid the seeds of their eventual doom. . . .

Thongor never knew how long his tour of the City of a Thousand Marvels lasted, for his mind, dazed and uncomprehending beneath the weight of horrors he was shown, at length refused to witness any more. But he was left with a grim and savage certainty that this Black City must be erased from the face of the world, if men were ever to dwell in peace and safety. Despite the awesome miracles of science the Wizards of Zaar had achieved—despite their magnificent mastery of the very forces of the universe —they had bent their unearthly arts to the domination and destruction of man, not to rendering his life easy and more comfortable.

For this grim reason, then, the city must be destroyed and the sorcerers who dwelt therein wiped out to the last man. Naught could be spared, if the world was ever to draw a safe breath again throughout the fullness of time.

Deep in his soul, the bronze giant vowed to his gods that were he fortunate enough to survive the perils in which he now walked, he would strive and would not cease from strife until he had pulled down all of this magnificent city in flaming ruin—even if he were to destroy himself in the great attempt!

And with all this cunning, Thongor's mind dwelt again on that mighty sea wall behind whose impenetrable barrier was, as yet, held back the imponderable and all-conquering fury of the Unknown Sea. Yet how could he—one man, and not a god—bring about the destruction of that gigantic wall?

106

In his tour of the workshops of hell, he had been shown a dull white powder refined after a thousand experiments from an unlikely combination of chemicals and elements. Within each dry granule of that innocuous-seeming powder was locked the titanic ravening fury of an earthquake. This most deadly and disruptive of all explosives was so powerful, he was told, that a mass of the whitish stuff no bigger than a man might gather into his cupped palms could demolish a ten-foot-thick wall of solid granite.

Deep within himself, Thongor pondered how he might escape the scrutiny of these sorcerers, retrace his winding passage through the labyrinthine ways of the mighty ziggurat, and gain a supply of the deadly powder wherewith to shatter the sea wall so that the overwhelming waves of the great ocean beyond might come thundering down to bury this dark city beneath their sprawling weight . . . even were he to die in the attempt!

One tremendous question repeated itself within his mind: *Was this the mighty purpose for which the gods had guided him to this dark place of hell?*

He thought of his beloved, whom he had not seen in many long days and empty nights. Never to hold her slim, yielding warmth within the circle of his strong arms again! Never to look down into the brave, clear eyes of his young son—to watch the lad grow and strengthen—to guide him through his youth with wisdom and courage and kingliness!

Was this what the gods had destined for Thongor the Valkarthan? Was it the will of heaven that he immolate himself on the pyre of Zaar—destroying the city, even if he must perish amidst the conflagration that consumed it? How could he know? Perhaps they were preserving him for some greater, more significant cause . . .

Yet what cause could be more urgent than the death of Zaar?

Busy with his dark thoughts, he had not been aware of the ways in which his captors led him. Now, as they stopped, he looked up at a mighty door of sheeted gold worked with flame-edged designs.

The masked magician pointed ahead.

"Now has the hour come, O Thongor of Patanga, when you must stand before the Nine Lords of Zaar in chains to receive their judgment . . . and to learn of the doom that has been set aside for thee!"

And Thongor's blood ran cold at the unholy, gloating glee that rang through the tones of the Black Archdruid.

What doom was this, so terrible that it raised this gloating mirth? What doom did Thongor face in the Hall of the Nine Thrones?

All too soon he was to know, and to taste the bitter cup of despair. . . .

CHAPTER 15

A KNIFE IN THE DARK

For thy black reign of wizardry
Draws near the end. It is too late,
Thou proud dark city by the sea—
For Thongor stands within thy gate!

And Jegga's Prince hath passed thy wall,
Great Zaar! He roams thy winding maze
And seeks to learn what doth befall
His friend amidst thy hidden ways.

—*Thongor's Saga,* XVII, 23-24

Shangoth swam in icy black waters, lost and totally confused in direction. Every time he tried to reach the surface of the rushing river, his hands encountered the low roof— too low for an air-space! His great lungs burned with searing pain, starved for air. His mighty heart labored like some overladen engine on the brink of breakdown. If he did not find a way out of this subterranean conduit—and soon—the roaring waters would bear on their frigid current a lifeless corpse.

A great portion of strength and breath had the Nomad spent in bursting the bars that blocked the way. For a long breathless eternity he had struggled to rend the mighty shafts of iron. Scaly rust cut and tore at his horny hands

The mighty thews of a giant swelled and writhed across his broad shoulders and mighty back. At last, with a surge of furious strength that left him shaken and nigh exhausted, the prince of the Jegga had fractured one of the ancient iron bars, shattering it clear from its socket. He had swum through into a black and lightless world of icy rushing waters—but no air! And if his bursting lungs did not soon drink in good air, they would force open his tight-clamped lips to drown in the bitter black floods of this River of Hell.

. . .

Light!

Light ahead of and above him glimmered faintly through the black-scummed waters! With the last ounce of strength, Shangoth put all the force of his massive shoulders and deep chest muscles behind a mighty surge that brought him to the surface.

His burning lungs sobbed in great draughts of fresh air, and for a moment he came to the brink of swooning from the sheer ecstasy of breathing once again.

But soon his laboring heart and heaving chest stilled. The roaring left his ears and his dazed mind cleared. He looked about him. He was at the bottom of a sheer-sided shaft some twenty feet deep, that plunged down from a barred grill into the rushing river-waters below. The sides of the shaft were beslimed with stinking refuse and nameless offal. For a moment he could not orient himself and sought vainly to understand the strange configuration of this narrow, filth-stained shaft. Then it came to him that, with a river rushing beneath their city, the Black Magicians of Zaar must have conceived of the idea of sinking shafts from the street level down into the subterranean conduits through which the river roared—for double use as storm drains, to carry away the rainwater that ran through the gutters of the dark metropolis, and as an easy method of garbage disposal. If this theory were correct, then one of the streets of Zaar lay directly above him!

But how to ascend a vertical twenty-foot shaft? He saw no handholds, no ladder. The walls of the black well were lined with that same smooth, vitreous substance of which the city walls were built, so there were no blocks of stone with interstices between them.

He surged up out of the water and set his broad shoulders against the lip of the shaft, bracing himself against the smooth, slimy wall by jamming his booted feet against the further wall. Once he was securely set, he inched his torso up the shaft a little, sliding his tough hide against the glassy stuff. Then he lifted one booted foot higher against the opposite wall, and braced himself in the higher position. Now he was entirely out of the water. He repeated the process again, gaining another foot or two . . . and again . . . and again . . . inching up the black well like some monstrous caterpillar.

It was actually less arduous than it sounds. For Shangoth was a huge man, and his massive body quite blocked the shaft. The only difficulty was that occasionally his shoulders slipped against the glassy surface and he slid part way back down the drain-shaft until his stiffened legs halted the descent. His body was soaking wet and befouled with the scum of the river-water. The shaft itself was slippery with rotting garbage, and many times during the interminable nightmare process of inching slowly up the tall shaft, he thought to fall back into the rushing water below, and lose all that he had gained.

Eventually, he reached the grill at the top of the stormdrain, and found to his vast relief that it was not bolted nor soldered down, but was set loosely atop the mouth of the well. From the amount of light that filtered down on him through the close-set bars, he guessed that the shaft-hole was set in a dark alley or enclosed place. He could hear no footfalls over the booming roar of the waters below, so taking a chance that no one was near enough to observe him as he emerged from the well, he pried the cover up and slithered out to lie panting on the stinking muddy cobbles of the street.

But time was of the essence. He could not permit himself to lie here in blissful ease, resting his sore and aching muscles, when he was still in instant danger of discovery. He staggered to his knees and set the heavy circular grill back in its grooved setting atop the echoing shaft.

Then, rising swiftly to his feet, he peered around. The narrow winding street was deserted and lit but feebly from a curious globe of pale fire that hung mysteriously in midair at the street-corner. Glancing about, he spied the ebon mouth of a shadowed alleyway some distance away and sprinted for it, gaining the safety of its relative darkness after his exposed position there in the middle of the street.

Then he examined himself. His harness was in tatters. Its buckles and ornamental badges had been scraped or torn away and the acid waters of the dark river had eaten the gilding from the leather. Of his supplies and accouterments and weapons, only his great ax and a slim-bladed dagger were left. Outside of sore and lamed muscles, and several raw spots where the shaft wall had rubbed away his tough hide, he was unharmed, but plastered from head to foot with stinking slime.

Alone, amidst a city filled with his enemies, Shangoth of the Jegga Nomads knew that he must be wary and take great care. A single false step might betray him. And surely, should some inhabitant of the city chance to encounter him in his present state, it would arouse suspicions in his mind.

Rain dribbled thinly down from a dark sky lit with intermittent flares of blue-white lightning. Shangoth wished for a heavy downpour, so that he might cleanse his body in the deluge. But with a little searching through the crooked alley, he found a rainbarrel beneath a roof-gutter, filled to the brim with fresh water from a recent cloudburst. With this water he washed his body clean of the refuse of the river-passage.

But what of his garments? Were any of the cityfolk to recognize his tribal insignia, they would wonder that a Rmoahal warrior of the Jegga Nomads freely strode the streets of their forbidden city. He must change trappings . . . and soon!

He followed the alley to its other end, which opened on a great square lined with the towering walls of some enormous palace or mansion. Carved gargoyles leered down at the square with snarling, stone-fanged maws agape. Globes of eerie phosphorescence shed an uncanny glow over the wet cobbles . . . and by their magic illumination, Shangoth, peering from the shadowed mouth of the alleyway, saw people bustling to and fro, busied on unimaginable errands. Among these were many blank-faced Rmoahal slaves, which was a relief to the Jegga Prince, who had feared that

111

even were he able to disguise his nation in borrowed raiment, he might rouse inquiry because of his race, which could not be concealed.

With narrow eyes he noted the comportment and garb of the Rmoahal slaves as they passed. They wore plain leather harnesses ungilded and devoid of precious stones or metals, save for the blatant insignia of their masters, badges of heraldic import which the slaves wore prominently displayed at shoulder-band, mid-chest and navel. He also observed that the Rmoahal slaves went from place to place without any interference from the Zaaryan guards posted at the entrances to the palatial buildings that lined the square. Indeed, the guards seemed hardly to notice them at all, and never in the time Shangoth covertly watched did they stop or question a single Nomad slave, nor ask to see identification or a travel-pass.

What he needed, then, Shangoth decided, was the slave-harness from one of these dead-eyed members of his race, so that he might pass amongst the men of Zaar unquestioned, while he searched out the place wherein the Lord Thongor lay prisoned. But for that, he must be patient and wait hidden in the shadows until one ventured near enough to the alley's mouth for him to seize and drag him within the shadows.

At long last, Shangoth's weary vigil was repaid. A tall, superbly-built Rmoahala emerged from the frontal gate of one of the palatial buildings and stalked across the nighted square toward the place where Shangoth lurked. His dull, dead eyes and features were totally devoid of expression as had been all those other slaves Shangoth had watched. The Jegga prince wondered briefly if the magicians fed their slaves some potent drug which destroyed their brains and made them mindless automatons. He noted that, even though this was but another zombie-like slave, the guards in the square paid him remarkable deference. Shangoth assumed this might mean his master was a figure of considerable importance within the Black City.

As the magnificent Rmoahal padded towards him, Shangoth scrutinized his raiment closely. It was somewhat more elaborate than the plain leathern harness worn by the others he had observed. The slave wore a voluminous

112

green cloak, and his trappings were of thick bands of emerald-green leather emblazoned with the characters which spelt "Vual" in the Lemurian script Thongor had been at pains to teach Shangoth and his fellows among the Patangan guards. The name suggested nothing to him. Loosening his dagger in its sheath, he crept yet closer to the alley-mouth.

As the dead-faced slave drew near, Shangoth made a hissing call just loud enough to rouse the attention of the slave, but not sufficient to be heard by the guards lounging across the way.

As he had hoped, the Rmoahal stopped—and turned toward the dark alleyway. Shangoth hissed again, and stepped forward so the slave could catch a glimpse of him.

"Come here!" he called softly.

Like some mindless robot of flesh, unable to resist a direct command, the mighty figure of the slave stalked forward into the dark mouth of the alley and vanished from sight.

He did not resist or cry out as Shangoth drove the thin blade through his heart.

Swiftly, Shangoth stripped the corpse of its harness, donning it himself, strapping his ax-belt high up between his shoulders, hidden by the cloak, and placing his worn and water-ruined trappings upon the unresisting body. Then he dragged the cadaver back down the length of the alley to the storm drain wherefrom he had emerged into the streets of Zaar. Luckily, this portion of the boulevard was totally empty. It was but the work of a moment for the powerful young prince to pry open the drain again and slide the cadaver down the shaft into the dark waters below, replacing the cover.

Then he straightened, forcing his features into the dead impassive mold of the other slaves of his race that he had observed in this city of darkness, dulling the keen luster of his eyes, and stalked off through the empty nighted street in a stiff-jointed stride that approximated the mechanical gait of the other slaves.

Now to find Thongor, wherever in this wilderness of black glass and sullen stone he was hidden. If, indeed, it could at all be done. . . .

All night Shangoth roamed the streets and tiers of Zaar. The people that he encountered paid but the slightest attention to him as he stalked through them, and that only a trifle of deference due, he assumed, to the status of his master—whoever "Vual" might be!

Although he wandered far, and loitered near many groups of men to overhear their talk, he heard but little concerning the Lord of the West. True, some of the inhabitants discussed in tones of gloating triumph the capture of Thongor the Mighty, but from all the talk Shangoth could overhear, none even mentioned the whereabouts of his imprisonment. A dozen times the Nomad wished he could engage them in seemingly innocent conversation and inquire casually if they knew where the barbarian was kept, but each time the thought crossed his mine, something kept him from it—some subtle intuition told him that Rmoahal slaves within the beetling walls of Black Zaar did not speak!

Other than this lack of definite information as to Thongor's dungeon, Shangoth's imposture was carried out with not a hitch. No one questioned his presence along the streets and squares of the city and no one ventured to bar his way, nor to approach him with questions.

Then, swiftly, came the end of his freedom.

A party of mounted guards on swift-pacing kroters came clattering through a column-lined arcade where Shangoth loitered, near dawn. It was with a distinct shock that the Jegga prince saw they wore robes of the same emerald green as his harness, and that the enigmatic word or name "Vual" was emblazoned on the browpiece of their hoods and the chests of their voluminous robes. They were armed with ebony shafts tipped with ivory bird-claws which clutched glowing crystals of strange power. Shangoth had seen such staves in the hands of the evil shamans of his people, before his father the great chief Jomdath had driven the vile warlocks forth. He knew with grim certainty that a glancing touch of those harmless-seeming wands could paralyze a man for hours.

He hoped they would pass him by with but scant notice. But Tiandra, it seemed, smiled on him no longer.

One of the mounted guards fixed him with a keen glance then reigned in his reptilian steed and called to his fellows

114

"*Ho!* Here he is. Phanthar, give the empty-brained lout your kroter—come!"

They reigned in about him. Still affecting the mindless mien and mechanical stride of the other slaves, Shangoth strove to stalk past them, paying them no attention. But it did not work. One seized his arm and bade him halt.

"Stop, you! The Lord Vual requires your presence —where have you been all these hours, you brainless fool? We've combed the streets since the Hour of the Cat!"

Shangoth halted, standing stiffly, not daring to look at the man who had addressed him, and wisely choosing not to reply.

One of the others laughed harshly.

"You know they cannot speak, Changthu. Come, drag the witless dead thing upon your kroter and let's be off—I may yet enjoy an hour or two of sleep before day breaks!"

Not daring to resist, ringed about by the guards, Shangoth permitted himself to be hauled into the saddle of one of the hissing kroters and woodenly rode off, accompanied by his guards. He had not the slightest idea of where they were taking him, nor of whom he was supposed to be, and deep in his heart he felt a leaden despair.

For all he knew, with every step he was being led farther and farther from his lord.

For all he knew, the guards were leading him into dire captivity, from whence he could not escape to lend aid to the imprisoned Thongor.

Yet he dare do nothing that was not seemly in one of these robot-like slaves. So he went forward dumbly, like an ox to the slaughter, and in his despair he had no notion that he was on his way toward saving the world.

Dawn broke, slow and sullen and fiery, over the frowning ziggurats of Zaar the Black City.

CHAPTER 16

THONGOR AT BAY

Now Thongor stands in chains alone
Midst judgment halls of ebon gloom,
While Mardanax from kingly throne
Hands down the grim decree of Doom.

—*Thongor's Saga,* XVII, 25.

They stood before the gigantic doors of sheeted gold whereon were worked the likeness of curling wavy-edged flames—such as might arise from the nether pits of hell itself. And one of the guards went forward to where a huge disc of jade hung suspended from a silver chain. He struck the center of this circle of pale jade and awoke a throbbing echo of bell-like sound that whispered away through thick shadows.

Slowly, the ponderous doors swung open . . . and Thongor stood on the threshhold of the great Hall of the Nine Thrones. Face grimly set, he strode forward into the vast echoing place of darkness, his footsteps ringing on the marble pave. The tremendous leaves of the portal swung shut behind him, closing together with an ominous brazen thunder like the crack of doom.

He stood alone in unbroken darkness.

Then, from the central pit, the fire-fountain blossomed. A great tongue of scarlet flame roared up from unseen depths below, painting the columned circular hall with leaping shadows cast by the nine tall thrones that were set in a ring about the pit of fire.

Gigantic shadows went crawling across the curving walls behind the nine great thrones, whereon was painted with uncanny skill a hellish mural which bore the portraiture of fantastic demons. For a moment he gazed on the painted figures of the mighty servitors of Chaos and Old Night—Lords of the Black Inferno such as terrible

Gamory and Zepar the Red, and Furfur who appears before mortals as The Hart with the Fiery Tail . . . dark Khil and fearsome Saleos who goeth mounted upon the Corkodrill . . . pard-headed Sitri with his gryphon-wings . . . and Beleth, the Rider on the Pallid Steed . . . shapes of unforgettable horror with eyes of sparkling crystal, limned upon the curved walls with incredible artistry in blazing colors that seemed to burn the very eyes!

Now scarlet light flooded the dim hall as the fountain of fire rose, shedding sheets of sparks. Guards led Thongor forth into the echoing hall, and brought him to a place near the well of flames, amidst the circle of towering thrones. And there they left him, vanishing in the shadows behind the thrones. He stared about him at the mighty chairs of colored stone, each looming atop its dais of glistening marble, and the tremendous backdrop of the mural whose demonaic figures leered down at him through the flame-shot gloom. Wet leather creaked as he surreptitiously tested his bonds.

Then came from without the vast doors of sheeted gold the ominous thunder of the huge jade gong, ringing in slow deep notes of solemn warning.

And one by one the Lords of Zaar took their places on the circle of thrones. . . .

Thither came Pytumathon to the seat of purple malachite, his gross, flabby bulk gowned in fantastic velvet and lavender silks. And war-like Maldruth, swaggering in scarlet and steel, a sardonic, mocking smile on his handsome, swarthy visage, as he gained the chair of sparkling crimson crystal. And quiet, bland Sarganeth of the Nuld in his voluminous robes, settling into the throne of gray granite, wherefrom he eyed the grim silent figure of the captive Thongor with mild and colorless gaze. And gaunt, mummy-like Xoth the Skull, his fleshless body wrapped in indigo cloth, feverish eyes burning from black sockets in his bald skull of a face. Mardanax the Black Archdruid reappeared, venomous emerald eyes gleaming with triumph, gloating through the eye-slits of his mask, taking his mighty place on the highest throne of black marble, and astly Vual the Brain, his tiny, shrunken, childlike body enderly cradled in the mighty arms of the blank-eyed Rmoahal slave, his enormous swollen brow and pinched elfin face hideous in their deformity, eyes of sharp black fire peered like evil gems at the silent Valkarthan as the zombie-like slave set him down carefully in his vast chair of lucent green jade.

The slave stepped back into the shadows behind the green chair, and the Wizards of Zaar looked down at Thongor where he stood, friendless and alone, in the very fortress of his enemies, ringed about with his greatest foes.

In solemn tones, Mardanax recounted the crimes of which Thongor was accused. He told in grave words how the Valkarthan adventurer had disrupted their carefully-laid plans against the Nine Cities of the West: how he had been the instrument of the destruction of their brother-druids of the Cults of Slidith the Lord of Blood and Yamath the Lord of the Flame, whose Orders he had broken and driven forth from Tsargol the Scarlet City and Patanga the City of Fire into homeless, wandering and scattered exile. He related in portentous tones how their brother, the Lord Thalaba the Destroyer, Prince of Magic, had met an ignominious death when Thongor had broken the siege of Patanga and sent the invading armies of the cities of Thurdis and Shembis fleeing from the field . . . and how a second of their brothers, the Lord Adamancus, Prince of Magic, had been whelmed and consumed in the clutches of his own demoniac servitor when Thongor had shattered and breached the very walls of his enchanted fortress to rescue the Princess Sumia and Shangoth of the Jegga Nomads. And he told, too, how their servants the Zodak Horde had been crushed before the iron legions of Thongor's ally, Jomdath of the Jegga, who now reigned supreme and unchallenged over the endless plains of the Rmoahal country.

Thongor knew that the only answer this magical tribunal could make to this long indictment would be . . . *death*.

And, doubtless, knowing full well the venomous rancor of these Black Magicians of Zaar, the punishment would be meted out in a manner lingering and artistic, a fiendishly-drawn-out death ingenious and coldly cruel.

But as the Valkarthan warrior stood silent and contemptuous before the judgment of his enemies, a flicker of hope yet wavered within his breast. It had taken every

118

atom of his powers of iron self-control to restrain his features in a mask of impassive rigidity. Almost had he gasped aloud with sheer unexpected shock when he had seen the Rmoahal slave who bore into the hall the dwarfed body of Vual the Brain—the zombie-faced Rmoahal whom he knew as one of his greatest friends: *Shangoth, Prince of the Jegga!*

How, or in what manner, Jomdath's son had come into this black city of necromancy and evil was beyond Thongor's ability to conjecture.

He had last seen the Prince of the Jegga when the invisible warriors of Zarthon the Terrible had closed the jaws of their cunning ambush about Thongor's men at the Hills of the Thunder-Crystals. At his last glimpse, Shangoth had been safely aboard the afterdeck of Thongor's floater . . . and then the invisible Zodak Nomads had seized Thongor and carried him off to the ruins of immemorial Yb the City of the Worm.

That was days and days ago, and many leagues to the north. Now had Shangoth transversed so vast a distance —and why? To attempt the rescue of the Lord of the West? Thongor's great heart warmed. Well did he know the devotion of the mighty Prince Shangoth of the Jegga, his friend. No other motive could have been imagined. Yet one terrible question burned within his brain, filling him with a nameless dread as he looked upon the rigid figure of Shangoth where he stood, brawny arms folded upon his mighty chest, staring blankly ahead with dull, dead, lusterless eyes.

Had the nine fiends of Zaar destroyed the mind and will of the Nomad prince with their vile sorcery—transforming him into a soulless robot of flesh, like the other living dead men who were their helpless slaves?

The judgment, when at last it came, was everything that Thongor had expected it to be. Upon his mighty throne of black marble, the Lord Mardanax terminated his lengthy, gloating indictment, and turned the matter of punishment over to the tribunal of the magicians.

"Now there remains only the manner of punishment," he said, and the Nine stirred in a quiver of anticipation. "You will recall, O my brothers, that I suggested a certain—*experiment*—at our last council, many days past?" His tones lingered gloatingly on the word, and his cold green eyes glimmered on Thongor with chill mockery. The Valkarthan stood in silence, his face as impassive as a mask of bronze. "An experiment which the Nine Books of Darkness call . . . *The Eternal Slavery of the Soul to Chaos?*"

Thongor did not know the meaning of this cryptic phrase, but the note of demoniac mirth, of unholy relish, in the smirking tones of the Black Archdruid raised the hackles bristling along his nape. He maintained his aloof, unspeaking calm, almost as if the topic were other than the means of his death. If the Nine Wizards of the Black City hoped to break his spirit, to bring him to his knees, grovelling at the foot of their thrones, they would not achieve this goal. He stood as unmoved as a statue of granite, contempt visible in the proud unyielding stance of his body.

". . . Since that time, my brothers," Mardanax continued in his purring, silken voice, "I have delved further into the procedures of this mighty ceremonial. Would you know further of it, lords?"

"Aye, O Elder Brother!" came the whispered reply.

"Never before in the seven thousand years of our dominion over this realm have we attempted this ritual. But soon it shall be performed—all *too* soon for you, O Barbarian!"

Thongor steadfastly made no reply, but maintained a grim and unshaken mien.

Mardanax laughed harshly. "I congratulate you on your courage in the teeth of the Unknown! But it is more due to ignorance than to bravery. Perhaps I should explain in simple terms precisely the manner of doom which we decree as your punishment. Let me explain. In this ritual, the Lords of Chaos are summoned into actual physical presence in the Temple of the Dark Powers. There, by a feat of potent magic, your spirit is to be torn from your living body and *fed* to the Chaos Kings . . . which act condemns your immortal soul to unending aeons of slavery in the service of the Masters of Evil, while your physical body, devoid of its animating spirit, becomes a mindless, drooling thing . . . a mere vegetable, incapable of intelligence or any act of will, but still sensitive to pain. And your body will indeed feel pain, O Thongor, for unending years of degradation and torment and bestial defilement . . . a slave in our hands even as your eternal spirit shall be a slave to the Dark Lords of Cosmic Evil! We will leave you with this pleasant picture to contemplate through the hours of loneliness that lay before you in your dungeon cell. Take him hence."

As Thongor was led away, he heard the Nine conclude:

"The Ritual of Summoning will be a mighty ceremony whereof the Lord Vual shall serve as Karcist or controller."

"Aye, Elder Brother. A great honor. . . ."

"Green Brother, you will for this ceremonial require the protection of that most potent of all amulets, the Grand Negator. Secure it from the periaptium and render it potent with a charge of unlimited absorption."

"I go, Elder Brother," the Brain hissed, summoning the black-eyed Rmoahal slave with a beam of thought.

Guards forced Thongor from the hall, stumbling towards a hidden door. He had hoped before leaving the Rotunda of the Nine Thrones to catch the eye of the mute Shangoth, to see if the Prince of the Jegga would—*could*—return his cognizance. But the guards bore him away before he could catch the Rmoahal's eye.

The door of his cell, a solid slab of steel broken only by a small barred window, clanged shut behind him. The guards had replaced his leathern bonds with shackles of cold iron wherewith they had chained him to a stout bronze ring in the wall. As the echoes of the steel door faded away, leaving him to darkness and silence broken only by the ceaseless dripping of water seeping from some unseen place, and the squeak and scurry of unza, the naked and scavenging little rodents of the pits, one phrase echoed and re-echoed through his mind.

The Eternal Slavery of the Soul to Chaos.

The malign intelligences that ruled this dark city had read well Thongor's stalwart spirit. Threats of physical torment could never wring a cry of pain from his lips, or bring the blackness and chill of despair to his mighty heart.

But *this* was a torment beyond the pangs of the flesh . . .

a torture of the very soul. And even Thongor the Mighty quailed beneath the dread of it, and it haunted his thoughts through the long hours he lay in chains alone amidst the dripping water, the chill darkness, and the squeaking of the rats.

CHAPTER 17

THE VOICE AT THE WINDOW

When bale-stars to their place return
To form a Sign within the sky,
When they were wont of old to burn—
Then shall the soul of Thongor die.

—*Thongor's Saga*, XVII, 26.

The stone wall of his dungeon cell was cold and wet and slimy against his shoulders. From somewhere, water dripped with a slow, maddening, repeated sound. The rustle and slither of unseen things came faintly to him, the squeal and scurry of tiny claws rasping against the stone. The unza were becoming bolder. And—coming nearer. Thongor set his jaw grimly. He had heard of prisoners who had been attacked by squealing, red-eyed hordes of the repulsive, naked rodents. And of prisoners eaten alive by the feral denizens of the dungeons—prisoners whose naked, gnawed bones moldered amidst rusty chains. Prisoners who had been . . . *forgotten*.

Such a death he could almost envy. But such would not be allowed to him by the Black Magicians of Zaar.

He wondered when his doom would come. The words of Mardanax had given no estimate of the interval that would befall before his judgment at the tribunal of sorcerers . . . and the terrible enactment of the sentence reserved for him.

Here, in this darkness, with the cold wet stone against his back and the slow drip of dank water punctuating the dead silence, he almost forgot what fresh air and the light of the open sky were like. His thoughts drifted as, despite the chill, the stench, and the discomfort of his chains, he dozed and dreamed. He thought of his mate, the dark-eyed princess, and his sturdy young son. He wondered what they were doing at this moment of time, and if they were thinking of him.

He thought of his distant homeland far to the north, the bleak and wintry Northlands of Valkarth that he had not seen since he was a boy. He saw again the face of his father, Thumithar of the Black Hawk People . . . his mighty bronze body cloaked in furs, battling the white glacier-wolves with long torches, howling his savage war-cry, black beard frosted with snow . . . and he saw again, in his mind's eye, the laughing faces and strong lean bodies of his stalwart brothers . . . and the quiet, beautiful face of his mother.

He remembered war-season, when the Snow Bear People swept across the frozen tundra to seize their fishing grounds. He remembered the ferocious battle on the black shore, when they battled with stone-tipped spears and bronze axes against the hordes of howling warriors, knee-deep in the black icy waters of Zharanga Tethrabaal the Great North Ocean. From crimson dawn to scarlet sunset they had fought, grappling hand to hand like savage beasts at the last, and when all was done, Thongor alone stood living on the grim beaches of death . . . panting, bone-weary, his naked body smeared with blood, ringed about with a core of dead foemen.

In that terrible battle had fallen his father and all of his bold, brave, great-hearted brothers . . . leaving Thongor to face a world of enemies alone, a boy of fifteen, friendless and kinless. He had buried his family there, digging up the black frozen earth with a broken ax, piling high the cairn of stones that would keep the wolves away. Then he had taken up the great Valkarthan sword his father had borne with so much honor, and his father before him, and countless ancestors dwindling back through time to the mighty hero Valkh the Black Hawk, seventh son of Thungarth of Nemedis, founder of Valkarth in the frigid Northlands . . . and with the great sword strapped to his side, he went forth to cut a red way through a world of savage enemies, hoping to find his place among men.

Down through the frozen passes of Mommur had he

123

ventured, to the sweltering jungle-lands of Chush and Kovia. For a time he had plied the trades of thief and assassin amid the splendid, barbaric young cities of the South. Then, condemned to a life of back-breaking labor in the slave-galleys of Shembis, he had broken his chains one night, strangled the brutal overseer whose lashing whip had cut long red weals across Thongor's mighty back, and led a slave mutiny to freedom. Stealing the very ship on which they had labored, hurling the crew and guards into the benches to take their places at the shackled oars, they had struck out for the high seas—for a life of freedom and piracy. For five years Thongor had been known as Black Hawk of the Sea Rovers, and his fighting men swept the Near Seas about the Gulf of Patanga with fire and sword, looting the richly laden galleys and setting them to the torch, while they sailed home to Tarakus the Pirate City, to guzzle red wine and swagger in stolen finery through the narrow lanes of that red, roaring kingdom of corsairs . . . fine, brave days they had been, filled with gold and glory, with blazing battle and high adventure!

And he remembered, too, how the captains of the Sea Rovers had turned against him when he slew their chief in an hour-long duel on the slippery quays under the streaming torches—how they had driven him forth and hunted him with the corsair fleets. For his clean, barbarian-bred manhood had revolted against the sadistic cruelty and torture with which the Pirate King had sought to extract information from captured sailors—and Thongor had struck the sneering, strutting monarch of the corsairs down. He had fled by night with half the Pirate City howling at his heels, to battle his way halfway across Ptartha to the docks of Zangabal. And there, to keep body and soul together, he had stolen food and gold—and made a friend. It was the young Zangabali warrior, Ald Turmis, who had persuaded him not to resume his career of thievery. Together they had shipped across the Gulf to Thurdis the Dragon City, when Thongor's iron strength and fighting skill had won him a place among the Guard in the scarlet leather of a mercenary.

For seven months he had fought the battles of Phal Thurid, the mad Sark of Thurdis, among the warriors of the Fourth Cohort. But again his fierce barbarian manhood

124

and pride had lost him a place among these city-bred men. For when a silken, pampered lordling welshed on a racing wager, Thongor promptly ducked him in a great bronze wine-bowl, and when he came up gagging, sputtering and half-drowned, Thongor set a length of clean Valkarthan steel through his guts. And he was off again, with half a city at his heels—for not only was the slaughtered lordling the scion of a princely house, heir to a title and a fortune . . . but also he was the *otar,* or captain, of Thongor's own company!

Thus had started the sequence of adventures that lifted the landless barbarian boy from frozen Valkarth to the highest throne among the Nine Cities of the West, beside the woman he loved. And if he had learned anything from his sojourn among the gorgeous cities, it was this: the simple code of manhood he had learned from the lips of his savage father was nobler, cleaner, more honorable than the laws of so-called civilization, where the whims of a foppish fool (be he of land and title) can outweigh reason, chivalry, manhood and honor.

He shrugged and stretched and yawned. And then he raised his voice in a deep-throated bellow that sent the rats squeaking and scrabbling for cover.

"Jailor! Ho—*jailor!* Gorm's blood, man, would you starve a warrior in these dank pits? Bring me *food!*"

At length his roars brought a yawning, shuffling turnkey who gaped through the close-set bars at him in walleyed astonishment. The fellow had heard pleas for mercy by the score from unfortunates locked in these cells—but never before one who raised a lusty bellow for a *meal!*

"Food?" he stammered, slack-jawed with amazement. "Man, have you gone mad from fear of what awaits—have you forgotten the sacrifice?"

Thongor laughed. "A man may die but once, friend. And, while waiting for it, a man can die of sheer hunger. Gods! It's been days—more days than I can count—since I last had a decent meal. Bring—me—*FOOD!*"

This last roar did the trick. The fat, foolish old turnkey went shuffling off into the dank dripping gloom at top speed, returning shortly with a huge wooden bowl of teaming hot stew, a slab of hard black bread and a beaker of thin sour red wine. It was hardly the spiced and princely affair Thongor was accustomed to in his own kingdom, but a hungry man cares little for frills and fancies. Thongor instantly fell too, while the turnkey gaped. He emptied wine-jug and bowl with a ravenous gusto you would not expect from one doomed to a hideous fate on the altars of Chaos—aye, and called for more!

Hours later (or was it days? For he had lost all sense of time in this dark, lonely place) he was awakened by an unexpected sound. The rasp of boot-leather on stone, outside his cell!

In one instant, Thongor snapped from deep sleep to icy alertness, straining every nerve to readiness. This was not the grumbling old jailor, huffing and slapping along in a jingle of keys. No. This was a surreptitious, careful step—— the step of someone who does not want to be heard.

Great muscles swelled across his broad, bronzed shoulders. Gods, but it was a terrible thing to be chained like this, helpless as a penned animal! Oh, to be free of the chains—to set his back against the wall of wet stone, with a good iron sword clenched in his hand—*then* let the devil-priests come and take him for their grisly rites and abominations! If they dared!

A face appeared in the barred opening in his cell-door. Little more than a black silhouette against dimness, it peered in at him. He, in turn, strained sharp eyes to make out the vague, shadowed features of—could it be——?

"It is I, Shangoth, lord."

"*Shangoth!*" The name was torn from him in an explosive grunt; then, dropping his tones to a hoarse growl, he said, "Gorm's blood, man, I was afraid these black devils had worked their devilish science on you, turning you into one of these mindless slaves!"

The blue-skinned giant grinned. "Nay, lord, my mind is my own still. I am here by a most curious trick of Tiandra." In swift, brief words, the prince of the Jegga outlined what had occurred in the past several days. How he had entered the streets through the underground river, and how he slew one of the zombie-like Rmoahal servants, exchanging garments with him, only to find himself mistaken for the slave of the Lord Vual the Brain, of the High Council.

"The dwarfed little fiend never deigned to actually look

126

a slave in the face, for to the Lords of Zaar we lesser beings are but as animals," Shangoth explained. "Hence when the guards he had sent looking for me brought me into his presence, I was able to take over the dead Rmoathal's duties without being questioned. 'Tis a stroke of good fortune, in a way, that the mind-destroying process leaves these poor brutes with no capacity for memory: otherwise, I would have been expected to remember my duties—which would have wrecked my imposture instantly! Instead, every instruction is repeated anew, and I was able to pull off the trick without discovery," Shangoth concluded, chuckling in his deep bass tones.

"Thanks be to the gods you are here!" Thongor rumbled. "In this cursed place, a friend or two could come in handy."

"Aye," Shangoth nodded soberly. "It was the shock of a lifetime when I carried the disgusting little dwarf into the Hall of the Nine and—saw you, my lord! Gods, I almost dropped the little beast! And I was afraid you would give me away by a start of recognition."

"I, in turn, tried to catch your eye," Thongor growled, "and when I couldn't, I feared they had made you into such as their other slaves—mindless cattle. But now you are here, Shangoth, can you get me out?"

Shangoth studied the door, then reluctantly shook his head. "Nay, sire, even my strength is useless. The door is shielded by black magic, and no force on earth could budge it without the key. But, hark to me for a moment. I am able to come and go as I like without question, for any that see me will recognize the insignia on my trappings and know me for a slave of The Brain, and think I am busy about some errand for my master. Hence I was able at least to find out where they had locked you away. And—since I must bear the hideous little monster in my arms everywhere it would go—I have listened to their councils and know their plans. The . . . the sacrifice is planned for tomorrow."

Tomorrow. . . .

"The hour is set by astrological computations," Shangoth whispered. "Some portentous constellation, whose stars have been far-scattered and wandering the skies for aeons, is now reforming into a potent and power-

127

ful sign emblematic of the ultimate, blasphemous rite in which they hope to render up your soul to the Chaos-Kings. But, even though I cannot get through the door to set you free, I have made a plan. It is dire and desperate, but better than nothing. . . ."

Thongor bent near as he listened to the soft voice at the barred window as it whispered the few words that stood between life and death for him. The plan was simple. It was also risky and dangerous to the point of suicide, but what could two men do against a mighty kingdom filled with enemies, except take a long chance and strike out boldly?

He agreed to Shangoth's scheme, and with a whispered farewell and a heartening word, the Rmoahal slipped from the window and was gone from Thongor's view, on careful, silent feet, leaving the Valkarthan brooding alone over the one last word that Shangoth had spoken—a word that summed up the rude, savage philosophy of Thongor's life:

"Courage!"

CHAPTER 18

BLACK ALTARS OF CHAOS

The stroke of Doomsday is at hand
For darkling Zaar beside the sea—
Thongor has burst his bonds to stand
With naked sword, unchained and free!

—*Thongor's Saga,* XVII, 27.

The temple of the Black Gods was a titanic hall of black marble where stupendous pillars like stone sequoias bore a vast dome of crimson crystal ninety yards above the tiled floor. The circular walls were ringed with rising tier on tier of stone benches like some infernal amphitheater, whereon in their rustling hundreds gathered the priests of Zaar to observe the fantastic spectacle of Thongor's doom.

In the center of this walled and dome-roofed amphitheater a colossal idol loomed up against the crimson light . . . like some supernal and malignant giant frozen into living rock, it stood, a graven Atlas of tremendous proportions whose cliff-like shoulders bore not one but *three* heads.

Beneath this triple-headed idol of Chaos was a row of nine varicolored thrones, and between the spread legs of the stone giant rose a cube of black marble ten feet high, glistening in the fiery glow of flaming lamps.

Standing atop the marble cube of the black altar, Thongor stood, his arms stretched out and bound with chains of gold that stretched to either side of the cube.

The Hour of Sacrifice was come!

Bronze bells groaned and trumpets screamed like brazen-throated harpies.

One by one, the lords and princess of Zaar took their places in the row of nine thrones.

Slobbering, obscene Pytumathon, gross in fantastic purple. Sarganeth of the Nuld in quiet, subdued gray. Bold, black-bearded, swaggering Maldruth in blazing scarlet. Lean Zoth the Skull, eyes burning with sick fanaticism, wrapped in robes of blue. Mighty Mardanax, masked and robed in ebon black.

And Vual the Brain, his dwarfed form and wobbling, hideously swollen head robed and hooded in emerald green, borne in the mighty arms of a dull-eyed, blank-faced Rmoahal slave that only Thongor knew as Shangoth of the Jegga.

A dull, moaning chant rose from the crowded stone benches that circled the titanic hall. It rose and ebbed, droning and roaring like the sea. The rite was begun. . . .

Now would come the test.

Could Shangoth's flimsy, desperate plan succeed?

Through the long hours of a day and a night, that question had scorched through Thongor's brain. Soon . . . *soon!* . . . would he learn the answer.

The Lord Vual had been selected for the high honor of performing the central role in the Ritual of Summoning. At a rasping, peevish command from his master, the mighty Rmoahal slave bore The Brain from his throne amid the Nine Wizards to the great pulpit before the cube-shaped altar whereon Thongor stood chained and helpless. Depositing the dwarfed form of the Green Magician on the stone podium, the massive slave stepped back and stood behind Vual, powerful arms folded upon his breast, his tall figure wrapped in the voluminous green cloak.

Vual made ready as all watched in an utter, breathless silence. As Karcist of the rite, it was Vual the Brain whose mind would serve as the medium by which a call should be sent from the massed thousands who lined the stone benches of the vast arena. Far, far into the lightless and unknown depths of space the mental summons would hurtle . . . beyond the very stars . . . behind the wall of curved, three-dimensional space that enclosed the mighty universe of stars like a hypersphere . . . deep, deep into the mysterious depths of the eternal and limitless Chaos-Realm that lay forever raging and impotent beyond the Walls of Creation.

Upon the stone lectern before the dwarfed enchanter lay a mighty book, locked with nine seals of red gold set with glimmering sithurls.

At the utterance of a potent Word, the seals snapped up and the huge tome lay open before the Karcist.

The pages of this enormous book were not fashioned of paper or parchment, vellum or leather, but of thin glittering sheets of foil, made from some unknown imperishable metal. For the supra-potent sigils and talismans written in these pages would sear and disintegrate any substance less durable. From where he stood, Thongor could see the complex figures etched upon the glittering leaves in weird metallic inks of scarlet, ebon black, sulphur yellow and searing indigo . . . the metal leaves, embossed with these phosphorescent designs, shimmered with an eerie halo of colored light that glowed with uncanny radiance . . . a flickering spectrum of magic illumination! The very air about the book of metallic leaves seemed to throb and seethe with turbulence, as if the terrific and potent sigils contained, locked within their very patterns, a force so colossal that it could be confined to the page only with enormous effort.

And Thongor knew the tome, knew those cryptic and pre-human symbols, for he had glimpsed its like once before, in the bastion of Adamancus.

This was *Sardathmazar, the Book of Power,* which unhuman hands had inscribed half a million years ago in the far and terrible land of mythic Hyperborea, aeons before the First Man was molded from the dust of the earth.

And Vual spoke, hands set upon the Book of Dreadful Wisdom, his piping, reedy voice rising shrilly through the breathless hush . . .

"I, the Lord Vual, Prince of Magic, Lord of Zaar, Master of the Nine Sciences, do invoke and conjure Thee, O Triple King of Chaos, by the Ineffable and Terrific Name of Power—IAO-THAMUNGAZOTH, before which Name the Elements of Creation tremble, the air is shaken, the earth doth quiver in her place, the sea runneth back into her secret deeps, the fires of heaven and earth are quenched, and all the Host of Spirits Terrestrial, Celestial and Infernal do quaver! Come Thou unto me, O Unborn One, by the Power of PAUMACHIA, ANAPHEXATION, HELIOREM, PRIMEUMATON, come, I command and beseech Thee, by the Bottomless Abyss of Everlasting Torment, by the River of Fire and the River of Blood, and by the Incomprehensible and Awesome SEAL OF TRIPLE CHAOS Itself, I summon Thee! Bathol, moving to Soluzen. Abreor, coming upon Ledrion. Malphas, dominant over Shaxphar!"

As the Lord Vual spoke on, repeating the terrible words of the grim Invocation, his voice weirdly seemed to change—to deepen in timbre, gathering strength and augmented power. Behind the dwarfed figure of the little enchanter, the blackrobed priests on the tiers of stone seats swayed and chanted in rhythm and unison with his words, and Thongor felt the skin of his nape and arms prickle with eerie premonition. Almost it seemed as if the mighty domed hall was filled with invisible currents of impalpable force streaming from the brains of the hundreds therein, linked and bound together by the controlling intellects of the Nine Wizards, and propelled and directed by Vual as the Karcist, or controller of the rite . . . the very air seemed to tingle with electric tension, as this mighty beam of mental force arrowed up from the surface of the earth and shot forth in a ray of probing thought, aimed at some hidden place beyond the stars. . . .

"Come, come, O Thou Mightier than the Gods . . . Come, by the Puissant and All-Powerful Name TOKTAH

131

TAVARONAKH, before which Name the spirits of the dead shrink back affrighted, and the hearts of the living weaken, and the Eternal Powers are made to quail! Come Thou unto me, O King of Night and Terror, by the Potency of ABIMESH, ZIO, ABLUTOR, BALDACHIENSIS, come, I summon and conjure Thee, by the Rune of Ko and the Sign of Ygg, come by the stupendous Forces of IRION, ORAZYM, SURGAT, NADAMIEL, come by the Star of Yrimid and the Nine-Sided Sigil . . . by the Black Monolith and the Scarlet Lake do I conjure Thee! Mathon, bind Raux. Zurgatha, rushing upon Phos. Raum, follow Aleth. Phaton, obey Yarnath!"

Now had the voice of Vual grown to superhuman depth and volume, as if the combined voices of hundreds spoke through his pale, distended lips. The monotonous, repetitive, pounding thunder of the ritual rose and rose in mind-numbing waves of sheer sound, beating against the Valkarthan where he stood atop the cube of black marble, dragging against his sanity and self-control as mounting waves of surf batter and drag against a mighty bastion of stone builded against the waves of ocean.

". . . Come, by the Words THAGLA, ARMISOR, ZALAY, GUTHAC, GUTHOR, TZAPHNIEL . . . Come, we await Thee O Lord of Ten Million Aeons . . . Khil, summon Frimost. Acorib, seize control of Axaxar. Alaoster, over lothoth . . . Come! Come! COME! COME!"

And then he saw It.

Far above him in the misty heights, were shafts of dim scarlet light struck down in broad rays through the cloudy crystal dome to strive and mingle with the thick ebon gloom . . . where the air seethed and thrummed with terrific currents of sheer Mind . . . *Something like a cloud of frigid blackness, taking form,* a whirling funnel of darkness, black as death, cold as the deeps between the space-worlds.

A breath of that cold wind struck Thongor, chilling him to the bone, cold as the wind that blows forever between the stars, as he stared up into the whirling funnel of blackness that was growing, growing, growing huger and more solid, and drifting down towards the place whereat he stood, chained and helpless.

Then it was that Shangoth struck.

From beneath the enveloping cloak of green, he drew his great war ax—and the mighty Valkarthan broadsword which Mardanax had taken from Thongor at his capture! Shangoth had found the sword in his wanderings through the citadel of Zaar, and had borne both weapons into the Temple, hidden beneath his voluminous green cloak. Now he raised his ax and let it fall in a terrific whistling stroke that severed the enormously swollen head of Vual from his shrivelled, thin neck—as a rotten fruit is struck from a twig!

Eyes still glaring with cold intensity of concentration—mouth still moving in spasms, forming unspoken words of summons and command, the hideously distended head of the dwarfed enchanter rolled to the foot of the Black Throne whereon Mardanax sat frozen—rolled to the foot of the black dais and thudded like dead meat against the marble step!

Spouting a sickly pale ichor from the raw stump of its neck, the shrunken, insignificant body slumped and fell forward, toppling from the podium before the blazing Book of Power; quivered, and lay still forever.

As if a knife-blade were drawn across a thousand shouting throats, the thunderous rhythm of the great Invocation was cut off. Silence crashed down in suffocating weight upon the awe-stricken multitude.

Roaring his deep-throated Jegga battle-cry, Shangoth sprang with a single great leap to the black altar whereon Thongor stood. The ax whistled again through the dark air, and the golden chains rang like tiny bells against the black marble as the blade clove through and severed them.

Thongor was free!

With a great booming cry of battle-lust and joy, the Lord of the West caught his own beloved broadsword as the Prince of the Jegga flung it sparkling through the air at him.

Now, with his mighty sword in his good right hand, he felt fit enough to do battle with the very Gods of Darkness.

Mardanax rose to his full height there upon the dais of the Black Chair, and extended his staff towards Shangoth. Bellowing his battle-song, the eight-foot warrior sprang to meet him—but a ray of green light shot from the tip of the

133

staff and bathed his mighty form in a flickering nimbus of pallid, throbbing force.

The blue-skinned giant froze motionless as a statue of graven stone!

Atop the black altar, Thongor prepared himself for one last magnificent battle against his enemies. But even as the muscles bunched in his long, powerful legs—even as he gathered his strength for a great leap that would carry him to the foot of the Black Throne—he felt himself seized in the grip of an eerie force, a tingling, electric coldness that probed down like a ray of darkness from the hovering spiral cloud that hung above him.

The frigid grip of a numbing paralysis held him motionless, unable to move. The sucking, gnawing cold benumbed his brain, dulling his mind, robbing the strength from his body . . . he felt as if cold hands grasped at the very roots of his soul!

For a long, terrible, endless moment this tableau held—Mardanax upon his throne, the Rod of Power extended—Shangoth the Avenger, frozen in the grip of the green ray—Thongor, held in the paralysis of the Dark Cloud that hovered above him, ready to suck forth his immortal and imperishable soul—

And then Mardanax *broke*.

The staff wavered, then fell, clattering against the ringing stone. The Black Archdruid sagged weakly against his throne, as if the strain of sustaining the green ray of paralyzing force had sapped some inward source of occult strength.

Shangoth recovered, shrugging off the weird power of the paralyzing force, and took in the situation at a glance. He whirled desperately to Thongor's aid, mind racing in a furious effort to think of some way of counteracting the dark power radiating from the Black Thing that hovered above the lone figure of the Valkarthan atop the altar.

And then his eye caught the glistening green talisman that still hung about the spouting stump of Vual's neck. In a flash, he recalled words overheard in a council of the Nine—"The Grand Negator, you will require the protection of that greatest of all amulets, Green Brother, if you are to serve as focus and Karcist in the mighty Ritual."

He snatched the green talisman from the corpse and hurled it through the air to Thongor in one desperate, last hope.

It caught on the Valkarthan's outstretched arm, looping about his wrist!

Like a breath of summery warmth amid the icy chill blasts of winter, the talisman's touch sent life and strength surging through Thongor. With stiff, still-numb arms he seized the dangling amulet and hung it about his throat where it dangled against his heart.

The paralysis of the dark ray left him. He shouted ly to Shangoth, and the blue-skinned giant whirled to charge the row of thrones, swinging his war ax lustily as he hurled like a human projectile among the powerful wizards who still sat stiffly, frozen with shock. Xoth the Skull went down, his gaunt skull-like head cloven to the brows before one ringing stroke. Shangoth leaped to the next throne, bringing his scarlet and dripping blade down upon the huddled, cowering gray-robed figure of Sarganeth of the Nuld, who squeaked shrilly, like a rat seized in the jaws of a cat, as the cold steel ripped deep in his vitals, and his life-force gushed from his body with the scarlet flood of hot gore. . . .

But still the black center of whirling cold hovered high in mid-air above the shrieking, stampeding throng. And as the mighty Lords of Zaar died, one by one, the Thing of Darkness grew as if it fattened on death, and was swollen and more solid with every stroke of Shangoth's scarlet sword!

Torn between the urge to stand beside his friend, and the deeper urgency of danger from this awesome and unholy Thing that the combined force of the Magicians of Zaar had brought down from the deeps of Chaos, Thongor hovered, caught in the grip of indecision.

And then tendrils of darkness writhed down upon him, cold tentacles of shadow whose icy touch bit deep as knives . . . he was caught up, dangling in the shadowy air . . . *he was being lifted into the Vortex of Darkness, and the black maw of Chaos gaped to receive him!*

As consciousness faded, as strength ebbed from his body and his mind shook and wavered like a candle-flame blown in a chill gust of wind, Thongor of Valkarth summoned every waning atom of dwindling life within him, gathered it and cast it forth in one mighty, despairing and thunderous cry of supplication—

"O Gorm, aid me! *Gorm! GORM*—"

Then darkness came down upon him.

CHAPTER 19

BATTLE OF GODS

The very Gods do heed his call,
And battle 'midst the storm-torn sky;
And now upon that sea-built wall
Hurl bolts of lightning from on high!

—*Thongor's Saga*, XVII, 28.

—And, out of darkness, light.

He came to himelf slowly. It was as if layer after layer of mind-swathing mist were gradually lifting from his consciousness. Groggily, Thongor lifted himself to his knees and stared about him.

All was shouting and tumult—priests running hither and thither in a mad, blind panic, or standing in little groups of two or three, staring at something above them with pale faces and glittering eyes wherein awe and terror blazed.

He looked up.

Looming a hundred feet into the air, Gorm the Lord of the Stars towered above the panic-maddened throng.

The titanic form of the god was like a stupendous, cloudy pillar of dim mist. His stern, kingly visage glared down at the tiny figures that fled and scampered to and fro between the shadowy columns of his legs. White wings grew from his temples beneath the cloudy mane of flowing hair and the long beard that poured down his mountainous chest like a cataract of dim shadows. His colossal breast and shoulders and arms, rippling with the thews of a giant, were cloaked in storm, and fiery flashes of lightning played about his majestic head.

It was of such unearthly and magnificent grandeur . . . a sight to strike awe into the heart of any mortal.

As he lifted up his face to the towering, shadowy figure of his savage god, Thongor's blood raced heady as wine in his veins, and he lifted his great Valkarthan broadsword in the warrior's salute to his king.

Above the shrieking tumult of the maddened throng, Thongor's deep-chested war-cry rose like a mighty trumpet-call. "*Hai-yah!* Thou Father of Gods and of Men! Hail unto thee, O Gorm, that thou didst not fail me in mine hour of deepest need!"

And in the depths of his mind, a great Voice uttered slow solemn words. "*Hail to thee, O thou Child of the North. In thy dream didst I tell thee that only in moments of Ultimate Peril to the very Universe may We take action in the World of Men . . . therefore am I come unto thee.*"

Thongor gazed away to where the Black Thing hung, baffled and cheated of its prey, before the colossal stone image of its triple self. It hung above the earth, dense as a thunderhead, cold as the boreal pole, roiling with mysterious turbulence, and . . . somehow, *incomplete*. Shangoth had struck off the head of the Lord Vual before the mighty Ritual was completed, and the Shape From Chaos had not fully taken on substance and being within this plane. But even in its half-formed state, it recognized its foe, one of the Gods of the Created Universe.

The Black Thing swept upon the shadowy god! They met, and the mighty hall was shaken to its foundations with the impact of that collision. The floor buckled and heaved: tiles snapped and splintered. Men staggered and fell.

Like a monstrous vampire bat, the shape of darkness sprang at the god's throat—

The dim, shadowy hall was flooded with blinding light, as if the noontide sun had flared into being within the arched curve of the crystal dome—as twin shafts of blazing white lightning sprang from the god's lifted hands to shower the Blackness with utter Light.

Thunder rolled. The walls shook. The vast hall was lit with supernal flares of flaming lightning, as the Lord of Creation and the Lord of Chaos were locked in stupendous and ultimate conflict! It was a scene to stun the imagination. The air seethed with the tension of ferocious energies released by the battling divinities of Heaven and Hell. Lightning blazed and flickered; the air was filled with a burning shower of fiery sparks. Great silver lamps were overturned, spilling pools of oil whereon roaring flames fed, adding to the swirling confusion.

Amidst the fury, Thongor spied his comrade Shangoth upon the daised thrones battling for his life. The Valkarthan could see even through the whirling confusion and drifting veils of smoke and sparks the bright flash of the Rmoahal's bronze ax as he held off an armed body of infuriated priests. As for the Lords of Zaar, they sat paralyzed with horror in their high places, looking upon the battling gods.

Thongor raced across the floor of riven tiles to lend aid to his embattled comrade. His great Valkarthan broadsword rose and fell, and rose again, its bright sheen stained now, and streaming with hot gore. Ere long had Thongor hewn a red path through the throng to Shangoth's side, and the two warriors fought back to back against the screaming mob of frenzied druids.

Thongor's sword cleaved skulls and lopped off limbs. Soon each stroke scattered droplets of blood on the smoky air like a crimson rain. Through the roar and thunder of battle, the shriek of the injured, the howl of the attacker, the bubbling groan of the dying, the iron music of blade on blade, his deep voice rang, chanting an old warsong of his barbaric people.

"Hot blood is wine for Father Gorm!
The War-Maids ride the wings of storm!
Our stout blades their red harvests reap
And thirsty steel at last drinks deep!"

The crimson murk of battle-lust rose to blind him with the old familiar berserk fury of war. He fought like a tireless machine, his bronze arm rising and falling, his black mane streaming in the tempest, the deep booming chant of his primal war-song ringing above the tumult and the carnage. The druids outnumbered the two warriors, but the sweeping scythe of the Rmoahal ax and the slashing fury of the Valkarthan broadsword soon eased the balance against them.

And then, quite suddenly, there were no foes about them, only the black-robed bodies of the slain heaped about. Thongor leaned on his great sword, panting, drinking in huge lungfulls of the reeking air, as his vision cleared.

But—what of the Archwizards?

In his first, frenzied assault—it seemed long hours ago—Shangoth of the Jegga had cut down three of the Black Lords of Zaar: Vual the Brain, Sarganeth of the Nuld, and Xoth of the skull-like visage. What had become of the others? He turned, eyes searching the row of thrones, to see gross, purple-clad Pytumathon sprawled obscenely in his mighty seat, his flaccid face pallid as wax. Perhaps, in an extremity of terror before the wild spectacle of battling gods, the overtaxed heart of Pytumathon had failed him . . . perhaps a chance blast of magic force had severed the strands of his life . . . but whatever the reason, the Purple Mage lay dead in his place of power.

But scarlet, sardonic Maldruth was very much alive. He had recovered from the shock of Gorm's manifestation, and now turned his attention to Thongor and Shangoth where they stood panting for breath amid the heaped slain. An ironic smile lifted the corners of his bearded lips and his black eyes laughed down at Thongor and the Jegga prince.

"Noble swordplay, my Lord of the West! 'Twas quite a spectacle . . . but now you face an adversary of somewhat different skills!"

Thongor eyed the tall, powerfully built figure of the Scarlet One without trepidation.

"Valkarthan steel can cut through scarlet robes as well as robes of black," he growled. "Come, red dog of Zaar, and I will show you the truth in my words!"

"I have no doubt you speak the truth, my primitive friend," Maldruth grinned mockingly. "But simple swordplay is so . . . crude, so . . . *basic*. Mine are rarer skills."

He lifted one strong hand and a strange ring caught the flickering light and blazed full in Thongor's frowning face. The ring of strange silvery-green metal was set with a bright gem—it was the ubiquitous sithurl, and it seemed the Black Magicians of Zaar used the mighty power-crystals as instruments in their dark sorcery even as

139

Thongor's realm planned to employ them in the cause of science.

A momentary numbness swept over Thongor's nearly naked body like a chilling breeze—swept over him and was gone. Whatever the nature of the blast of magic Maldruth had hurled at the Valkarthan, it had no effect upon his iron strength. He lifted his dripping sword toward the surprised Prince of Magic and laughed harshly.

"Try again, red dog! It takes more than mere spells to halt a warrior!"

Again the sorcerous ring flashed with numbing brilliance. And yet again. Beyond a brief and passing chill, the talisman had no power over Thongor. He greeted each futile attempt with a ringing laugh, then strode grimly forth towards Maldruth with sword at the ready.

This was perhaps the first time in his bloody, cruel and supernaturally prolonged existance that Chaos Magic had failed the Scarlet One. And it shook him—more deeply than Thongor might guess. For the swaggering, bold, sardonic Lord of Zaar—behind his swarthy, handsome, heroic façade—was naught more than a cheap bully and a rank coward, when stripped of his eerie magical skills.

And now that façade cracked—badly. Globs of cold sweat glistened on his brow; his eyes gleamed uneasily, searching from side to side like a trapped rodent. Again the Lord Maldruth raised the sithurl-studded ring to bathe the Valkarthan in a beam of magic force.

Shangoth's deep laugh rang out. "The talisman!" he boomed, pointing to the strangely carved amulet of green jade-like stone that dangled against Thongor's bronzed chest. The Valkarthan glanced down at it—the sigil Shangoth had torn from the headless corpse of Vual the Brain—the sigil he had slung about his neck—the Grand Negator, the Lords of Magic called it! This was the source of the magical protection that shielded him from the power of Maldruth's ring-weapon!

And Maldruth's eyes were drawn to the curious, all potent talisman as well. Naked desperation flamed madly in his glaring eyes, that flashed no longer with lazy, languid and cat-like malice. He knew that he was a dead man.

Trembling with terror, he glanced madly from side to side, seeking for a way out—some means of escape from the need to face the grinning Valkarthan warrior-king with naught but cold steel alone, man to man.

But escape there was none.

Mouthing a vile oath in a voice that shook a little, the Red Prince tore his gilded rapier from its gemmy scabbard and aimed a wild blow at the blood-bedrabbled barbarian. With a deafening *KLANGG* of steel meeting steel, Thongor deflected the blow, and swept Maldruth staggering to one side with the force of his defence.

Now they set to it, while Shangoth watched grinning widely, leaning on his nicked and dulled ax.

Sword rang on sword like stricken gongs. Thongor's point ripped across Maldruth's tunic from shoulder to shoulder. The bright fabric, severed, fell away, baring the Scarlet One's naked chest. Then Thongor gave him a slight cut on the bare flesh, almost playfully.

As they fought on, Maldruth panting and gasping from the unwonted exercise, sweat began to glisten on his heaving chest, and his fine raiment became stained and dishevelled, ripped here and there with the keen point of Thongor's mighty blade, dribbled with blood that leaked down from a score of scratches and small wounds.

Now Maldruth's handsome visage was distorted and pale with rage. Panic blazed madly in his wide eyes. His lips were drawn back in a rictus of fury that bared his teeth in a silent, gasping snarl. His headdress was cut away and his black hair became a wet tangle, falling into his wild eyes.

If it had not been pitiful, the unmanning of Maldruth would have been amusing. Almost at any time from the beginning of the match, Thongor could have ended it. But, for a time, he played with his frantic, trembling, now-half-naked and completely outmatched adversary with the lazy malice of some great tawny cat.

It became too much even for Shangoth's primitive sense of justice. "End it, lord," he said quietly.

Terror flamed up madly in Maldruth's goggling eyes. "No—*no!*" he screeched shrilly.

Thongor put a foot of steel through his guts and set his booted foot against the feebly-twitching body, withdrawing the soiled blade with an impassive expression on his face.

Amid the confusion of the duel, unseen by either Prince

Shangoth or Thongor, who were both intent on the humbling of the Scarlet One, a black-robed figure crept from the highest throne where it had sat frozen all this while.

Like a dim shadow it passed through the hall and faded into the gloom behind one of the mighty pillars.

A black-gloved hand fumbled for a hidden catch, and a secret opening yawned. The robed figure hovered for one long moment on the threshold, gazing back, to see Thongor dispatch the Red One.

Cold eyes of emerald venom glared fervidly through the slits of a black mask—then vanished, as the dark figure of the Black Archdruid of Zaar disappeared in the secret passage. The door swung to behind him and he was gone.

Aloft, above the row of thrones, the battle between the Gods of Light and Darkness, too, had ended, the Black Cloud of Chaos deluged with the ravening bolts of blinding flame from the hands of Father Gorm. At first the shape of darkness drank in the dazzling beams of brilliance, absorbing the light within the shadow . . . but at the last, the Thing From Beyond, drenched in torrents of utter light, gave way. Its subtle internal structure of balanced forces was no longer able to sustain itself.

The very air shook with a terrific implosion as the Black Thing collapsed inwards upon Itself and disintegrated into nothingness.

The shock of the implosion shook the room, and slowly—slowly—the colossal stone image of Triple Headed Chaos crumbled on its foundations and fell!

In mid-air, the three heads broke from the stone neck with a grating cry of tortured rock. The snarling, laughing raging visages of rock crashed down upon the row of stone and crushed them to powder.

The titanic limbs detached themselves from the leaning toppling torso and fell like an avalanche of shattered stone—pouring down upon the milling guards and priests.

The air was filled with rock-dust. Columns were toppling like storm-shaken trees. The walls split—a web of black cracks zigzagged from top to bottom. The building was coming down. And, in the whirling dust-motes and roar of breaking, crumbling masonry, the vast and shadowy figure of mighty Gorm faded from sight and was gone.

Amid the shattering masonry, dazed by the swift whirl of events, Shangoth staggered, white with dust from head to feet, dragging his mighty bronze ax. Thongor seized his arm.

"Quick! How do we get out—*move*—the whole thing's coming down over our heads!"

The urgency of Thongor's words drove through the dazed wits of the Nomad. The two sprinted across the heaving, bucking slabs of broken stone that had been the smooth tiled floor. Far ahead, through the dust and thunder of collapsing walls, the great bronze leaves of the door gleamed in the light of distant fires.

Then—shock upon shock!

The dome of scarlet crystal shattered into ten million shards of broken glass and hurtled down like a rain of deadly swords. Suddenly the sky was filled with flickering bolts of green-white fire—the horizon was laced in a burning net of lightning bolts—and then the mighty temple walls gave way and came thundering down in a stupendous storm-cloud of whirling dust, and the lone, small figures of Thongor and Shangoth were hidden from view. . . .

CHAPTER 20

BESIEGED BY LIGHTNING

Break, wall, and shatter, stone! Set free
The thunders of the waves that sweep
The wizard city 'neath the sea
A thousand fathoms buried deep.

—*Thongor's Saga*, XVII, 29.

was like the end of the world.

From nowhere, without warning, a mighty fleet of silvery airboats emerged from the dense clouds that overhung the sky, and floated above the canyon-like streets of the

City of Magicians. And from the needle-pointed prows of the weird flying craft, where enigmatic structures of gleaming metal could be seen bolted to the urlium hulls, came fantastic bolts of dazzling lightning . . . lightning from heaven, directed by human intelligence!

The hissing, seething rays of electric fire swept over the frowning walls of Zaar and hordes of guards were burnt to cinders in the crackling fury of the fiery bolts.

Then the ships floated down over the streets, striking with their mysterious destructive rays at guard-citadels and key positions. Walls and buildings were shattered into atoms at the touch of the blinding bolts. Towers collapsed, blocking whole avenues with landslides of rubble. Wooden roofs and sheds burst into flame as the flickering lightning beams touched them in passing. From a hundred sites, smoke from burning buildings came whirling up to fill the sky with sheets of sparks and dense clouds of choking smoke.

Thom Pervis had fulfilled his grim duty with savage devotion. When the invisible warriors of the Zodak Horde had seized Thongor in their ambush at the Hills of the Thunder-Crystals, the last words of the Valkarthan had been a terse order to the commander of the Air Guards to bear back to the mage Iothondus the load of power-crystals they had unearthed before the jaws of the trap were sprung

Although the grizzled old daotar would rather have lost his right arm than desert the Sark-of-Sarks in such dire straits, duty lay clear before him and, with tears burning his eyes, he had unflinchingly obeyed Thongor's last order The fleet had risen from the embattled hills and he had guided it west away across the full length of the Lemurian continent, to Patanga and home, at the very greatest speed of which the floaters engines were capable.

In the long, weary days and nights that followed his arrival in the City of the Flame, Thom Pervis had watched with gnawing impatience as tireless Iothondus toiled almost without rest or nourishment. Under the spur of the Empire's urgent need, the mild and quiet-voiced young natural philosopher had become a grim-faced, unwearying martinet, flogging his corps of assistants on, hour after hour, day after day, laboring far into the night to cut the sithurls, mount them on their brackets, and see them tested

144

and installed at the prows of the sky navy. Then, armed with a destructive power never before at the command of mortal men, the vengeful Air Guard of Patanga had raced back across the stormy skies of old Lemuria to arrive at the broken walls of the dead city of Althaar, where the Jegga Nomads lay encamped. Aboard the fleet had come Zad Komis, the Lord of the Black Dragons, with half a thousand seasoned warriors from Thongor's own guard, also the Princess Sumia and young Prince Thar as well, the princess white-faced and wordless in her despair and terror over the unknown fate of her beloved mate.

Jomdath, the old chief of the Jegga, had told them of his conquest of the Zodaki—and grudgingly, sadly, he had imparted the sad news that Thongor was not to be found, although the ruined city of immemorial Yb had been ransacked by his Rmoahal warriors. The fate of Thongor remained an unsolved mystery. The old chief had spared the slim, silent, courageous girl and kept his own suspicions to himself. Deep in his loyal heart, the old warrior was convinced that Thongor lived no more.

But regardless of the whereabouts of the Valkarthan, the place of the enemy whose machinations lay behind all their present difficulties was certain. There was no question in the minds of Sumia or Zad Komis or Thom Pervis that the foe was *Zaar*. And, although perhaps too late to come to Thongor's aid, they could at least avenge his murder. And, the two daotars grimly swore, it would be a vengeance such as the world would remember for a thousand years.

Hence had the war fleets of Patanga hurled their flying legions against the towering black walls of Zaar of the Magicians. And thus was the most ancient city of the world come to the last hour of her terrible and bloody history.

The fleet of Patanga ringed the city in and flashed above its walls and turrets. Under the heavy cover of storm-clouds, they had descended upon the black metropolis of magic without being detected. Now they struck in a blazing attack whose ravening fury brought death and destruction roaring through the streets.

In the cabin of the flagship, old Jomdath of the Jegga directed the aerial assault. Thom Pervis and Zad Komis knew nothing of the City of Magicians, but the savage war chief of the Blue Nomads knew the dark city all too well. For a thousand years the Wizards of Zaar had been the enemies of his people. Now he guided the attack with some measure of grim satisfaction in his bloodthirsty, barbaric heart.

The great Temple of the Chaos Lords he picked for the prime target. From the weird flames that shone up through the arched dome of crimson crystal, he guessed some blasphemous and evil ceremony was taking place within the unholy precincts: so he directed the bolts against that citadel of the Black Gods first. His words were flashed to a signalman on the afterdeck of the commander's ship. Within seconds, flags burst from the superstructure in multicolored streamers, and the Air guardsmen commanding the other vessels of the Patangan fleet read the command from the signal flags, according to a prearranged code.

A shower of lightning bolts descended upon the temple, and beneath the blazing beams of dazzling destruction, the very walls of the age-old structure burst asunder. With a thunderous roar, the temple dissolved in a landslide of rumbling stone and was gone, hidden in a tremendous cloud of dust and smoke.

Building after building received the full fury of the lightning guns. And building after building was shattered to atoms in the explosion. Within mere moments of the first assault, the Black City had become a fiery holocaust wherein panic-maddened mobs swept through rubble-strewn streets.

Never in all her dark and kingly chronicle had the City of Magicians known such an hour. Impregnable due to her massy walls of black stone, invincible, from the supernatural arts of her wizards, she at last tasted the inevitable wine of defeat, and found it bitter.

And what of her vaunted magical defenses and weaponry, with which her black-robed masters had planned to sweep the world with conquest and tumult? They availed for naught. The enemies against which Zaar was armed, and watchful, were armies of the land—not the air. Her far-seeing modes of vision, but one of which was the Black Archdruid's All-Seeing Eye, were turned to eternal and unwearying survey of the great plains—not the cloudy skies above them! She had failed to foresee that new eras brought new methods of war. She had failed to change with the times. Sunk in apathy, despising all other realms, confident in her own superiority, her overconfidence had now brought her to this terrible and disastrous hour, when the triumphant fleets of young Patanga swept above her blazing streets, lashing her crowds with scourges of lightning-fire.

As for the mighty weapons of black magic wherewith she was armed, they demanded certain time for preparation—a certain interval of forewarning—and time had run out.

The proud, hawk-like eyes of Jomdath of the Jegga were fierce with a warrior's joy as he watched the conquering fleets of Thongor's air navy victorious over the ancient enemy of his people.

And then his eyes flashed!

Ahead, glassily reflecting the flickering lightning beams as they probed the detonating masonry of the city below, a mighty rampart of black substance caught his eyes.

The sea wall. . . .

There it stood, that great bastion that held back forever the icy waves of Takonda Chann the Unknown Sea. The titanic wall of black marble towered above the City of Magicians like some colossal structure raised by the hands of captive giants, or the ramparts of some fortress of the gods.

Jomdath spoke the words that doomed Zaar.

Colored banners broke from the superstructure of the flagship, their coded sequence reiterating his grim directive.

And now the lightning guns turned their supernal fires against the beetling wall of black marble. Bolt after bolt went sizzling across its glassy surface. With terrific impact, the stored mega-ergs of sun power locked within the mysterious sithurls poured out against the vast structure.

For a long, long moment it seemed as if that ocean-defying rampart was built so strong as to resist even the thunderguns of Patanga.

But then Jomdath seized the right arm of Thom Pervis in a mighty grip. "There! Do you see?"

A crack ran shivering through the black marble.

The colored banners were withdrawn, and again went

streaming forth in a certain sequence. Now ship after ship focused the lightning rays against that one slight breach in the stupendous wall.

It widened.

Glittering slabs of surface marble were shattered and shorn away by the probing beams; they went quivering through the air like thick black motes silhouetted against the white blossom of utter flame that clung to the wall—the focus-point of a score of searing beams of ravening fury.

The blasting rays bored in—deeper—deeper.

Now lesser cracks spread from the main breach. A web of cracks zigzagged across the blistering, crumbling surface of the sea wall. Above even the roar of burning buildings from the city, and the droning roar of the lightning guns, arose a new sound. A note of menace. A dull, deep, growing, rumbling sound as of gathering thunders.

The ominous rumble was followed by an unearthly shriek of stone tortured beyond endurance, stone splintering!

And the Sea Wall fell!

The central portion of its mighty curve swelled outwards and broke with a thunderous roar—burst into a million huge shards of riven stone that went whirling through the stormy air. And in its place a solid wall of water flooded through the gigantic gap.

The massy weight of water struck the earth. It came down in the suburbs of Zaar, where from of old the lords and princess of the magical metropolis had taken their ease amidst the lilied languor of their palaces.

The palaces were crushed like paper toys beneath the tread of a giant. And the giant walked on, toward the city itself.

For many generations of man, that wall had held the ocean-giant back. But now the wall was burst, and the giant set free. And he went howling and roaring down upon the city of his foe. With slapping hands he smashed flat the man-built structures that stood before him.

The sea was loose; like an avenging monster, howling with elemental fury, it thundered forth upon the winding ways of Zaar—as the whole wall was torn away and shattered in a flood of ruin.

The impact of the weight of water shook the unstable

earth. A titanic foam-crested wave swept across the peninsula and drowned the Black City beneath its crushing weight, and in its rush it smashed apart everything that stood in the path of its irresistible advance.

Only the towers of Zaar still stood above the roaring waters, and one by one, as their foundations were ground to dust or swept away by the raging, foaming fury of the flood, the black towers toppled slowly into the seething waters and were gone.

The wave broke in thunder against the hills that rose beyond Zaar, at the edge of what had been the river beneath the city. Now all was a plain of roiling, muddy waters.

The earth shook before the giant's tread as he stomped the city down. With a thunderous shock, a black chasm ripped open across the base of the promontory, where it was joined to the main continent. The mighty crack in the earth spread—widened—and the waters poured in a titanic waterfall over its edge, thundering down to the volcanic core of the earth.

Within moments the very tongue of land where Zaar had stood since the first days would be swept by the waves and would founder, sunken a hundred fathoms beneath the triumphant waters of the unconquerable ocean . . . grim prelude to the eventual cataclysm which would overtake all of Lemuria in aeons to come, when the mighty continent itself would be drowned beneath an ocean that would someday be named, with unintentional irony, the Pacific—the "Peaceful."

And then a mighty cry broke from the lips of Zad Komis. "There—atop the hills!"

They followed his pointing arm, and Sumia cried out in a sharp, unbelieving cry of hope, *"Thongor!"*

And it was he. For when the mighty temple had collapsed in ruin, Thongor and Shangoth had raced forth into the streets and there had pried up one of the iron grills that covered a storm-drain—plunging into the subterranean river only a little time before the probing lightning-beams of Patanga had turned the black metropolis of magic into a seething holocaust of blazing flames. They had swum forth by the same route by which Shangoth had made entry into the city—out through the broken grill in the wall, and forth

149

from the river's brink, climbing the hills to their crest to watch the stupendous spectacle of the Fall of Zaar. Thus, from the vantage point of the hilltop, they had stood in safety while the colossal sea-wave swept the city to ruin and thundered across the shallow valley to break against the hills almost at their feet. But now the sharp eyes of Zad Komis had glimpsed the mighty Valkarthan and his comrade, and the flagship drifted down to hover above the crest of the hill. A rope ladder was dropped to them and within moments Thongor swung up over the rail to the afterdeck and swept his beloved into his arms, to crush her against him in a mighty embrace and to seal her warm lips with one long rapturous kiss, while all about them Shangoth and his mighty sire, and the lords and warriors of Patanga split the air with a great shout of salute and triumph.

"*Hai—Thongor!* Sark-of-Sarks and Lord of the West!"

And thus was The Last Battle fought—and won—or so it is written in the Lemurian Chronicles.

* * * *

EPILOGUE

WHEREIN THE TALE HATH ENDING

". . . Yet over all did Thongor triumph, for the immortal Gods themselves were leagued with him in war against the Dark Ones. Armed with the very lightnings of Heaven, Thongor the Mighty broke asunder the black bastions of Zaar and the ancient City of Magicians, with all its evil wisdom and dark science, sank beneath the overwhelming waves of the unconquerable sea and was gone forever from the knowledge of men. And thus did the worshippers of the Third Lord of Chaos perish utterly from the earth, and thus shall the Servants of Darkness ever fail and fall, in whatever age or land they strive to dominate . . . for is it not written in *The Scarlet Edda* that Light shall forever be victorious against the Dark?"

—The Lemurian Chronicles

And thus the vengeful ocean broke
The grim Black City's age-old reign
And freed Man ever from the yoke
Of Druids drowned beneath the main.

And Thongor with that stalwart friend
Who sought him long in lonely quest,
Their perils done . . . at journey's end,
Turn homeward to the distant West.

—Thongor's Saga, XVII, 30-31.

IT IS ENDED.

APPENDIX

GLOSSARY OF CHARACTERS MENTIONED IN THE LEMURIAN BOOKS

(NOTE: Major characters, with the exclusion of the gods or other mythological beings, are given in alphabetical order with a brief explanation of their role in the series. Where necessary, the individual books in the series are referred to by the following abbreviations: TAG—*Thongor Against The Gods;* TCM—*Thongor In The City of Magicians,* etc.)

ADAMANCUS. One of the Nine Wizards of Zaar, slain by his own magic when Thongor entered his tower to rescue Sumia and Shangoth, in TAG.

ALD TURMIS. A young swordsman of Zangabal who served with Thongor as a mercenary in the legions of Thurdis and later companioned him during many adventures. When Thongor became Sark-of-Sarks he elevated Ald Turmis to the dais of Shembis as its Sark.

ARZANG POME. The cruel Sark of Shembis who leagued with Phal Thurid to conquer Patanga in TL. He was slain the following year when Patanga whelmed the forces of Tsargol.

BARAND THON. Daotar of the Fourth Cohort of Thurdis in which both Thongor and Ald Turmis served as mercenaries. He was later created Sark of Thurdis when the House of Phal Thurid came to its end.

CHANGTHU. A warrior of the Black City in the service of Lord Vual the Brain.

CHARN THOVIS. A young recruit who served in the Black Dragons and saved the life of Thongor when his party was ambushed at the Hills of the Thunder-Crystals in TCM. Thongor made him Otar of a hundred warriors and a *kojan* of the empire.

CHUNDJA. A warrior of the Jegga attached to the retinue of Shangoth who accompanied his prince to Patanga where he became a member of Thongor's personal guard.

DALENDUS VOOL. Baron of Tallan. A treasonous noble of Patanga, secretly an agent of the Black Druids of Zaar.

DIOMBAR. The Singer of Nemedis. A poet of the First Kingdom whose *Song of the Last Battle* preserves a first-person account of the Battle of Grimstrand Firth wherein the Dragon Kings were broken and The Thousand Year War was ended. Diombar's *Song* is quoted in part in WL.

PRINCE DRU. Sumia's cousin, the third peer of the realm and a member of Thongor's councils. Also hereditary Daotar of the Patangan Archers.

DRUGUNDA THAL. Sark of Tsargol, slain by Thongor when he escaped from the arena with Karm Karvus in WL. Yelim Pelorvis the Red Archdruid assumed the dais at his death.

EODRYM. Wise old hierarch of the Temple of Nineteen Gods in Patanga and one of Thongor's chief advisers.

FALVOTH PTAR. A young Air Guardsman, pilot of Thongor's personal yacht. He was slain in the Zodaki ambush at the Hills of the Thunder-Crystals.

GORCHAK. The old shaman of the Fire-People, a tribe of

neanderthaloid Beastmen who captured Thongor, Sumia and Karm Karvas in TL, and from whom they are rescued by Barand Thon.

HAJASH TOR. The would-be conqueror of Patanga. As Daotarkon of Thurdis, and later, when leagued with the Red Archdruid of Tsargol, he twice attempted to whelm the City of Fire. He was slain by Prince Shangoth of the Jegga at the close of TAG.

HASSIB. Chamberlain to the court of Drugunda Thal, Sark of Tsargol.

HIMOG THOON. An alchemist and priest of Yamath in service to Vaspas Ptol the Yellow Archdruid. He devised the black vapor of madness wherewith the Archdruid planned to destroy the Host of Thurdis in TL. Lord Mael slew him in the first moments of the revolt that freed Patanga from the Druids.

HOSHKA. A chieftain of the Zodak Horde, leader of the ambush party that seized Thongor at the Hills of the Thunder-Crystals.

INNELD. Eldest daughter of Lord Mael; a handmaiden to Princess Sumia.

IOTHONDUS. The Sage of Kathool, a young natural philosopher in the service of Thongor who designed the sithurl-weapons wherewith the Air Guard demolished the City of Magicians. Later, he adapted the sithurls as a power-source to drive the engines of the airboats of Patanga. He is remembered as one of the wisest of The Wise, the first and greatest Nephelos of Lemuria.

JAIDOR. A great hero of Nemedis the First Kingdom of Man, and father of Thungarth of the Star Sword who whelmed and broke the Dragon Kings at the Battle of Grimstrand Firth.

JELED MALKH. Heir to the House of Malkh in Thurdis the Dragon City and Otar of the company wherewith Thongor served during his time as a mercenary swordsman. Thongor slew Jeled Malkh in a duel described in WL, which occasioned his outlawry from that city and set in action the sequence of events which led to the Valkarthan's fateful meeting with Sharjsha the Wizard.

JOMDATH OF THE JEGGA. Mighty Rmoahal warrior, Lord of the Jegga and Father of Prince Shangoth, whom

Thongor encounters first in TAG. He later became the first Sarkon of the Five Hordes, and the most powerful ally of Patanga.

JUGRIM. A member of Shangoth's retinue who joined Thongor's personal guard with his Prince.

KARM KARVUS. A Prince of Tsargol the Scarlet City and heir to a noble house under the persecution of Drugunda Thal. He met Thongor when they were both imprisoned, awaiting death in the arena of Tsargol. Escaping together, they became firm friends and comrades. Karm Karvus later became the first Daotar of the Air Guard. When Patanga conquered the Scarlet City in TAG, Thongor raised Karm Karvus to the Sarkdom of that city.

KHORBANE. A warrior of ancient Nemedis who fell at the Battle of Grimstrand Firth. One of the Sons of Thungarth.

KOGUR. A Beastman whom Thongor encounters in the jungle country of Kovia in TL: the chief of the Fire-People.

KONNAR. A warrior of Nemedis, mentioned in Diombar's *Song of the Last Battle*.

LULERA. Younger daughter of Lord Mael, a handmaiden in the service of Sumia the Sarkaja.

LORD MAEL. Grizzled old Baron of Tesoni near Patanga, one of Thongor's chief peers and advisors, and a leader of the revolt wherein the City of the Flame was set free of the rule of the Fire Druids.

MALDRUTH. The Prince of Red Magic, one of the Nine Wizards of Zaar; slain by Thongor in a duel in TCM.

MARDANAX. The Black Archdruid and supreme Lord of the City of Magicians. He alone escaped the destruction of Zaar.

MUGCHUK. A Beastman, or Gunthya, of Kovia; one of the tribe of Fire-People encountered by Thongor, Karm Karvus and Princess Sumia in TL.

NARJAN ZASH DROMOR. One of the Ommya befriended by Thongor and Karm Karvus when they were imprisoned in the Lost City of Omn in TL. It was he who slew the immortal *morgulac*, Xothun, and saved the life of Thongor.

NUMADAK QUELM. A Yellow Druid, highest of Vaspas Ptol's henchmen; he succeeded his master to the Archdruidship after he was slain in Mael's rebellion, and later conspired with Arzang Pome of Shembis, Hajash Tor of Thurdis, and the Red Archdruid of Tsargol to whelm Patanga. He was slain by Thongor in battle before the gates of the Scarlet City, and with him died the Yellow Brotherhood.

ONGUTH. A *Gunthyan* of the Fire-People of Kovia who rescued Karm Karvus and the Princess Sumia from the embrace of the cannibal trees, only to imprison them.

OOLIM PHON. The old Alchemist of Thurdis who discovered the secret of urlium, the magic metal that makes the flying airboats of Patanga possible. He first succeeded in isolating the synthetic isotope in the Year of the Kingdoms of Man 6999, eight years before the opening of WI, and constructed the prototype airboat which Thongor stole in making his escape from Thurdis in the same novel.

ORVATH CHOND. Sark of Patanga and father of Sumia Sarkaja. The last Sark of the House of Chond, his dais was usurped by Vaspas Ptol the Yellow Archdruid.

PHAL THURID. The Mad Sark of Thurdis. Driven near the brink of madness by the sorcery of Thalaba the Destroyer, an Archimage of Zaar, and tempted in dreams of world conquest by the ambitious Hajash Tor, the last Sark of the House of Thurid sought to seize the Sarkdom of Patanga as the first step in his conquest of all Lemuria, but died when Thongor broke the Siege of Patanga. He was succeeded to the Sarkdom by Barand Thon when Thurdis became part of Thongor's empire.

PHANTHAR. A Zaaryan warrior in the service of Vual the Brain.

PHONDATH THE FIRSTBORN. In Lemurian myth, the First Man who was created by the Nineteen Gods at the beginning of The Thousand Year War against the Dragon Kings from far and fabulous Hyperborea. His sons founded Nemedis and the First Kingdoms.

PYTUMATHON. One of the Nine Wizards of Zaar, slain when the City of Magicians was demolished by the air fleets of Patanga.

QUONIDUS OF YB. An ancient philosopher of nature, one of the worlds' first *Nephelim,* or scientists. Iothondus quotes from his works in TCM.

RAMADONDUS VOTH. The only member of the Nine Wizards absent from Zaar when the Black City was whelmed and sunken beneath the waves of Takonda Chann the Unknown Sea. He had taken the place of Sarganeth among the Nuld.

RORIK OF THE AX. A Jegga warrior who joined the personal guard of Thongor along with his Prince, Shangoth, and Jugrim and Chundja.

SARGANETH OF THE NULD. The Gray Prince, one of the Nine Wizards of Zaar. Shangoth slew him shortly before the City of Black Magicians was destroyed.

BARON SELVERUS. Lord of Athnome near Patanga. A member of Thongor's council of advisors, one of the highest peers of the Sarkdom.

SHANGOTH THE NOMAD. Prince of the Jegga Horde and son of Jomdath. It was the Rmoahal Prince who accompanied Sumia on those of her adventures chronicled in TAG. When Thongor rescued them from the tower of Adamancus of Zaar, the Jegga warrior laid his ax at the feet of the Valkarthan in token of an oath of homage. From that hour he has been one of Thongor's staunch friends and comrades and a member of his personal guard.

SHARAJSHA THE GREAT. The mighty Wizard of Lemuria was one of the great mages of Zaar, but turned from the evil ways of the Black City to dwell in a subterranean palace beneath the Mountains of Mommur centuries before he persuaded Thongor to join in his quest against the Dragon Kings. It was Lord Sharajsha who re-created the Star Sword with which Thongor broke asunder the Black Citadel and brought doom to the last survivors of the reptilian sorcerers who sought to open a Door to Outside wherethrough the Lords of Chaos might gain entrance into Creation. One of the mightiest magicians of the Elder World, he aided the young empire of Patanga and when he passed to the Shadowlands he left his great Grimoire and Testament in the keeping of the Patangan Sarkons forever.

SSSAAA. The Lord of the Dragon Kings who led the

handful of his people who survived the fall of the Black Keep at Grimstrand Firth to their new home on the isles of the Inner Sea. He it was who sought to open the Portal to Chaos of the Night of Destiny. Thongor of Valkarth brought his unnaturally prolonged life to an end when he whelmed the Isles with the Star Sword in WL.

SUMIA. The only child of Orvath Chond, Sark of Patanga, whose throne was usurped by Vaspas Ptol. Thongor and Sharajsha aided her to escape from Patanga, where they had gone for the second stage of the creation of the Star Sword; the Princess of Patanga accompanied them throughout the adventures that culminated, in TL, with the overthrow of the Fire Druids, whereupon she wed Thongor and became his Sarkaja, in the Year of the Kingdoms of Man 7008. The tenth month of that year saw the birth of their son, Prince Thar.

TENGRI. A shaman of the Jegga Horde who plotted the exile of the rightful chief, Jomdath, but was himself exiled by the chief when Thongor rescued him.

THALABA THE DESTROYER. One of the Nine Wizards of Zaar who acted as the secret power behind the throne in Thurdis, to further the progress of Zaar's master-plan against the West. His life ended when Thongor broke the Siege of Patanga and ruined the schemes of world-conquest which Thalaba had implanted in the brain of Phal Thurid.

PRINCE THAR. Tharth ko-Thongoru—known as "Thar"—is the only son of the mighty Valkarthan and his mate, the princess Sumia. He was born in the tenth month of the Year of the Kingdoms of Man 7008, and is six years old at the period described in TCM.

THOM PERVIS. Warrior and nobleman of Patanga who became second Daotar or commander of the Air Guard, when Karm Karvus relinquished that post to assume the Sarkdom of Tsargol.

THONGOR OF VALKARTH. The greatest hero of all Lemuria was born at Valkarth in the Northlands in the Year of the Kingdoms of man 6982. He became a homeless wanderer at 15, the sole survivor of a mighty battle between his people, the Black Hawk clan, and a powerful foe, the Snow Bear tribe. Precise dates are lost, but Thongor was about seventeen when he reached the

157

cities of the South. From 6999 to 7002 he roamed from city to city as thief, assassin, and wandering adventurer—ending as a slave on the galleys of Shembis, from which he escaped in a slave mutiny at the age of twenty. For the next four years he roved the high seas as one of the pirates of Tarakus. He was driven from the Pirate City when he slew the monarch of the corsairs in a duel and wandered North to Zangabal, where he met a young swordsman named Ald Turmis who persuaded him to enlist with the mercenaries in Thurdis, whither Ald Turmis was bound. Thongor served in the Fourth Cohort of that city for seven months, his daotar being that same Barand Thon whom he later created Sark of the Dragon City. Near the end of that same year, 7007, he was forced to flee from Thurdis, making his escape in the stolen prototype floater which Oolim Phon had perfected. The remainder of his career has been chronicled in the Lemurian books in detail. At the period of TCM he is about thirty-two.

As founder of the Golden Empire, he became a legendary hero to his Imperial descendants and was later deified. In the pre-Sanskrit *Puranas* from which I have adapted the basic plot-structure of the Lemurian books, he is remembered as *Mahathongoyha* (Thongoyha the Great), a divine hero. To the early Saite Period Egyptians of the pre-Dynastic era, he was *Tahon,* a god of warriors. His descendants ruled as kings for a quarter of a million years.

THULAN HTOR. A warrior of Thurdis whom Thongor slew when he stole the airboat and made his historic escape from Thurdis.

THUMITHAR. The father of Thongor, a direct descendant of Valkh of Nemedis, founder of the Black Hawk people of Valkarth.

THUNGARTH. Son of Jaidor of Nemedis and leader of the expedition which went up against the Black Keep in the battle of Grimstrand Firth wherein, armed with the glory of the Star Sword, he whelmed the Dragon Kings and brought The Thousand Year War to its close. Among his seven sons was Valkh.

TOLE PHOMOR. An Otar in the legions of Tsargol the Scarlet City who served with the Arena Guard at the time when Thongor and Karm Karvus were imprisoned therein.

VALKH THE BLACK HAWK. Seventh son of Thungarth of Nemedis, founder of Valkarth *(Valkh's garth* —Valkh's holding) and father of the Black Hawk people from whom Thongor and Prince Thar are descended.

VAR TAJAS. A warrior of Thurdis who rode a zamph in the racing arena and lost. A wager on his winning was the cause of the fateful duel between Thongor and Jeled Malkh, the Otar of his Hundred.

VASPAS PTOL. The Yellow Archdruid, head of the Fire Druids of Patanga who worshipped Yamath the Lord of the Flames, an aspect of the Triple God of Chaos. The evil influence of Zaar was allied with the Yellow Brotherhood, but when Orvath Chond, father of Princess Sumia, died, Vaspas Ptol sought to seize the throne by marrying the Princess. He became so maddened with the lust of power that he broke with Zaar, whereupon the Black Magicians, working through Thalaba the Destroyer, set Thurdis against Patanga in War. When Thongor broke the Siege of Patanga and Mael overthrew the Yellow Druids in rebellion, Vaspas Ptol was hurled to his death from the walls of the City of the Flame. Thongor spared but exiled his successor, Numadak Quelm.

VUAL THE BRAIN. One of the Nine Wizards of Zaar; he was slain by Shangoth of the Jegga in the Temple of Chaos.

XOTH THE SKULL. Another of the Nine Wizards who met death in the Fall of the Black City.

XOTHUN. A *morgulac* who artificially prolonged his life for centuries through a form of vampirism. A brilliant *Nephelos,* or scientist, Xothun held the entire population of Omm the Lost City in the jungles of Kovia helpless beneath his power, and preyed off the people of the Lost City for untold generations, until he met his death as described in TL at the hand of one of his slaves, Narjan Zash Dromor.

YELIM PELORVIS. The Red Archdruid of Tsargol, head of the Red Brotherhood who worshipped Slidith, another aspect of the Triple Lord of Chaos. He shared rule of the city with the Sark, Drugunda Thal, until Thongor slew the Sark, whereon he ruled alone. In 7008, Hajash Tor and Arzang Pome, together with Numadak Quelm, took refuge in Tsargol, having been driven from their lands by Thongor the Victorious. The following year they combined forces and sought to destroy Patanga in war—an attempt chronicled in TAG.

YGGRIM. A warrior of Nemedis, one of the heroes who fell at the great Battle of Grimstrand Firth, as told in Diombar's *Song*.

ZAD KOMIS. A noble who had served in a high position in the legions of Patanga during the Sarkdom of Sumia's father, Orvath Chond, but was exiled when Vaspas Ptol seized power in Year of the Kingdoms of Man 7007. When Thongor set Patanga free of the grasp of the Fire Druids, Zad Komis returned and became daotar of the Black Dragons, Thongor's crack regiment of Veterans.

ZAFFAR. A wizard of ancient times who built the great palace which later became the Temple of the Fire God in Patanga, and, still later, was reconsecrated by Eodrym as Temple of the Nineteen Gods. More of an alchemist than a sorcerer, Zaffar experimented with the power of the mysterious Flame that has burned from the beginning of time in the unknown crypts below the Temple. It was Zaffar who constructed the secret stair by which Thongor descends to the Cavern of the Flame in the first chapter of TCM.

ZANDARLA THE FAIR. A Queen of ancient Patanga, famed for her dazzling beauty, who ruled the City of Fire thousands of years before the age of Thongor.

ZANDAR ZAN. The Black Thief of Tsargol, commissioned by the Four Conspirators in TAG to steal away Princess Sumia and the infant prince, as a means of luring Thongor into their power. The Thief of Tsargol's plans went awry and he met his death at the hands of Thongor as described in the concluding chapters of TAG.

ZARTHON THE TERRIBLE. The great war chief of the Zodak Horde and master of immemorial Yb the City of the Worm. Jomdath slew him when the Jegga Horde overran and conquered the Zodaki warriors and their ruined city.